with gratitude,
Linda

DAWN THROUGH THE SHADOWS

LINDA ANNE SMITH

Also by Linda Anne Smith
Terrifying Freedom

DAWN THROUGH THE SHADOWS

LINDA ANNE SMITH

Dawn Through the Shadows

Dawn Through the Shadows is a work of fiction. Names, characters, places, and incidents are the products of the author's imagination or are used fictitiously. Any resemblance to actual events, locales, or persons, living or dead, is entirely coincidental.

Jacket and interior design: Erik Mohr/Ian Sullivan Cant (madebyemblem.com)

ISBN: 978-0-9949295-4-9

To all who accompany others toward freedom in Love.

PART ONE

CHAPTER 1

Andrew Covick shifted on the undersized chair of the coffee house, crossed his leg and tapped his thumb on the small table.

A young man, his hand on the empty chair across from Andrew, asked, "May I take this?"

"No, I'm expecting someone." Andrew glanced at his watch. *Two more minutes and I'm gone,* he thought.

~

The call had been unexpected: the Reverend Theo Augustine O'Rourke wanted to meet for coffee. The two had parted ways over fifteen years ago and, until now, there had been no attempt on either side to connect. Theo, so he said, was passing through on business and "thought he would look up an old friend." But Chicago was not where they parted company nor were they ever friends.

Traffic noise and a blast of cold air indicated the arrival of more customers. Before Andrew saw his face, he knew Theo had arrived. Black trench coat, the collar lifted up to protect from the wind. Andrew watched as Theo smoothed his thinning hair and scanned the room. A big man always, Theo had filled out even more in a decade and a half, but his face was unmistakable even with his widened and sagging jowls.

Theo caught Andrew's eyes and made his way through the cramped tables and chairs, unbuttoning his coat as he came.

"I would have recognized you anywhere!" said Theo as he shook Andrew's hand and clapped him on the shoulder. "I see you've already ordered. Would you like a refill? Something to eat?"

Andrew declined both and Theo went to the counter to place his order.

Andrew sipped his coffee and continued to observe Theo. Black shirt with a cardigan? No, not Theo. He wore high-clerical garb: a black, tailored suit with a stiff white collar encircling his neck; crisp, white cuffs extending from his jacket sleeves just far enough to reveal his silver cuff-links; and a starched, black vest that lusted for a pectoral cross.

Theo returned, sipped some coffee and bit into a scone.

"How did you find me?" asked Andrew.

"The internet."

"So you're just passing through Chicago?" Andrew picked up his mug and leaned back in his chair.

"I'm here on business. I've been appointed to the Vatican committee for the International Festival of Young Adults."

"So there's a Vatican committee now."

"Yes, for a while now. We provide expertise to the local Church organizing the festival and oversight as well." Then, as if justifying his position, "Really, why should every host country have to 'reinvent the wheel' when we have a solid template?"

"Unless the wheel itself needs innovation. You know, the original wheel was a pottery wheel."

Theo shot a glance at Andrew, but let the comment drop. He chomped down a few more bites of his scone, took a sip of coffee and popped the rest of the pastry into his mouth. "I just made a deal with Secure Star Insurance and discovered it's the company you work for."

Andrew's back tensed and a long-latent twitch jolted his shoulder.

Theo sipped his coffee and smiled. "When I checked out the website for Secure Star and saw your name as HR director, I couldn't believe it! Out of touch for so many years and, once again, the IFYA has brought us back together." Theo laughed. "Those were the days . . . I-F-Y-A . . ." he sang off-key to the tune of YMCA.

Andrew did not share such pleasant memories of the I-F-Y-A, neither the adapted lyrics sung at the festival nor the source of the acronym: the International Festival for Young Adults. He wondered if Theo set up this meeting to flaunt the perpetuation of the IFYA or his rise within the hierarchical circles of the Church. Or was Theo completely obtuse to the seriousness of their disagreement years ago? Whatever the case, Andrew had already reached his threshold of civility for Reverend O'Rourke.

"I'd better be going," said Andrew. "I have a meeting in twenty minutes." He rose and picked up his parka.

"Always hard at work," said Theo as he stood. "Who knows, with Secure Star's involvement in the IFYA, we may meet again!" He shook hands with Andrew and put on his coat.

The men exited the coffee shop and walked off in opposite directions.

CHAPTER 2

"You're home early."

Andrew, hunched over the table, nursed a cup of tea and stared blankly at a strip of calligraphy that adorned the wall. "I took the afternoon off," he said, not turning to greet her. His shoulder twitched.

Rebecca rarely saw this side of Andrew. They had been together for several years and married for three. Andrew was easy-going, slow to react, and tended toward the longer view, but was never a brooder.

"Are you feeling okay?" Rebecca walked over and began to massage his shoulder. It twitched again. "Did you pull a muscle?"

Andrew closed his eyes and lowered his head.

"What the hell is going on?"

"Hell just walked back into my life," said Andrew.

"Who?"

"The Reverend Theo Augustine O'Rourke."

Rebecca continued to massage Andrew's shoulders, trying to loosen the taut ropes of muscle that seemed impervious to her touch. Over the years she had learned to wait. Andrew's story trickled out like a slow, spring thaw. With each retelling of past events, new details were added. As their lives merged, the framework of his life took form and she began to understand the empathetic man who had reached out to her years before. However, Theo O'Rourke?

"O'Rourke? I don't remember you talking about a *Reverend Theo Augustine O'Rourke*," said Rebecca, mimicking Andrew when she repeated the name.

Andrew smiled at her imitation. "It's more what he represents. I met him at college."

Rebecca pulled a couple of wine glasses from a cupboard. "Well, you must have made an impression on him, otherwise, why would he have bothered to look you up?"

"To gloat? I don't know."

Rebecca uncorked a bottle of wine while Andrew recounted their brief conversation at the coffee shop. "I've decided to pay a visit to Secure Star's upper management and see what's up," said Andrew, shaking his head.

"It may be a lot of hot air."

"I doubt it. Theo was rather pleased with himself." Rebecca sat next to Andrew with the glasses of wine and put her arm around his shoulder. "I thought I'd put the IFYA behind me years ago and now to be even remotely entangled in it is depressing."

"Was Theo part of that Proclaimers of Christ group?"

"Not directly. It all began at college . . . "

CHAPTER 3

Andrew had applied to several universities but a Catholic college in northern California offered a good business program and he'd received a scholarship. The latter clinched the decision: his parents were in no position to help financially. So, at eighteen, Andrew left the quiet suburb where he had been raised and went upstate, prepared to dive into his classes and look for a part-time job.

Andrew hadn't been there a month when he saw a professor crossing a campus green space. Head bent forward as he walked, the professor drew heavily on a cigarette and exhaled forcefully through his nose. He forged ahead like a steam engine, as though he couldn't keep pace with his racing thoughts. No one else seemed to take notice, but Andrew couldn't take his eyes from the oddity.

"Quite a sight."

Andrew startled and looked over at the young man who stood beside him.

"The Mad-Hatter."

"What?" said Andrew.

Nodding toward the man, "The guy there? We call him the Mad Hatter."

"Who is he?"

"One of the English profs. If he didn't have tenure, he'd be gone. A real 'nutter' as the Brits say."

"Have you taken any of his courses?"

"No. Wouldn't waste my time." Then, extending his hand, "By the way, I'm Richard. You new here?"

"Andrew," he said as he shook hands. "And yes, this is my first year."

Richard, Andrew soon discovered, was in his fourth year. He was tall and attractive, but more than that, confident and good-natured.

"There's a group of us getting together for a barbecue this evening. You're welcome to come." He gave Andrew a small flyer with directions to a room in the student centre complex. "Bring a friend if you like."

"I'm just getting settled. I don't know many people yet."

"All the better. This will give you a chance to make some friends." He extended his hand again and as they shook, he said, "Until tonight."

"Yeah, maybe . . . we'll see."

"The food's great," Richard said as he walked away.

Later that day Andrew glanced at the flyer and considered his tight budget. A free meal or extra study time. The food won out.

~

Andrew had just entered the student centre meeting room when he heard a voice call out, "So, you decided to join us!" Richard approached him smiling warmly, "Come on in and I'll show you around."

The meeting room was on the ground floor and opened to an enclosed patio. As they walked about, Richard introduced Andrew to several freshmen who self-consciously sipped their beverages and made attempts at small talk. The "newbies" were partnered with friendly young people who, like Richard, had attended the college previously.

"Oh, I see someone else has arrived," said Richard, scanning the entrance area. Pointing off to the side, he said, "Go, pick up something to drink and join the others."

Andrew looked over to a table where cans of soda chilled in a large bowl of ice. Feeling awkward standing alone, Andrew made his way to the table. As he edged past small groups of the newly acquainted, he picked up snippets of their conversations: "I just spent three hundred dollars on books for that course!" "My roommate snores like a bull." Andrew chose a cola, popped open the can and was walking toward a bench against the wall when another student joined him. "Hey, what brings you here?"

"To be honest . . ." Andrew held up the can of soda and thumbed over to hamburgers grilling on the barbecue.

The young man laughed, his smile extending to his cheekbones. "Gets you every time." He extended his hand, "Micah, Micah Baker."

"Andrew Covick." His pale skin intertwined with Micah's mocha shade as they shook hands. Micah's kinky hair was braided away from his face in rows that extended to the back of his head. Lithe and slender, he easily crossed his legs on the bench as they sat.

"You look like you're new to the city," remarked Micah.

"It's that apparent?"

"A hunch."

"And you?"

"Born here, other side of town—an hour and a couple of bus transfers to the college."

Micah, Andrew soon discovered, was following the Liberal Arts track.

"What do you do with that?" asked Andrew.

"Learn to think . . . so my parents say. I'm giving it a shot. What about you?"

"Business."

Just then Richard called out to them. "Come on over, guys. We're going to begin a few icebreakers."

Fifteen minutes later they were back at the bench with an addition, Mei-Lien Zhang.

"Might as well relax until the line thins out," she said.

Enticed by the aroma of the freshly grilled hamburgers, Andrew's stomach growled. But Mei-Lien was right: standing in line wouldn't get them food any faster—the tables were mobbed.

"So, you're from China," said Micah, continuing a conversation they had started during one of the icebreakers.

"My parents are. I was born in the US."

"You live in the city?" asked Andrew.

"My parents are professors here."

"Shit!" exclaimed Micah. "Now that's local."

"What do they teach? " said Andrew. "Maybe you could put in a good word for us."

"This is why I hate talking about my parents."

Andrew couldn't tell if she was serious or joking.

"Well, your secret is safe with us, right, Micah?"

Micah raised his eyebrows, "What *do* they teach?"

"Math and chemistry—graduate level," said Mei-Lien with a hint of a grin.

"Okay, we're done. You can go eat somewhere else," said Andrew. Mei-Lien laughed.

"What are you studying?" asked Micah.

"Pre-med. I want to be a doctor."

Micah whistled.

Andrew grabbed Micah's shoulder and said, "Micah is here to learn how to think, I'm here to do business and you're into medicine. We'll make perfect study partners! Mei-Lien, you keep us healthy, I'll manage your finances, and, Micah, you can write all the term papers, you know, like the nursery rhyme: healthy, wealthy and wise!"

"Good luck with that idea," laughed Mei-Lien.

"I'm already out," said Micah.

Richard seemed to spirit out of nowhere. "Hey, guys, don't you want the burgers while they're hot?"

Once through the food line, the three ate quickly. Micah had to catch a bus before it stopped arriving every twenty minutes, Mei-Lien had an early curfew, and Andrew needed to finish reading articles for a class and prepare for a job interview.

As they left, Richard handed them a flyer for the next event. Since leaving home, Andrew finally felt connected with a group of people outside the classroom. And the food was free!

CHAPTER 4

Weeks went by interspersed with several events hosted by Richard's hospitality club: pizza and movies, table tennis and hotdogs, and the like. With his course load and new job at the campus bookstore, Andrew could squeeze in little more than these social events. Being on such different academic tracks, Andrew rarely met Micah and Mei-Lien in the corridors, so he looked forward to catching up with them at these gatherings. Richard always joined their trio at some point, followed shortly after by another senior, Casie, who steered off Mei-Lien for a period of time. When these leaders included themselves within their group, Micah would excuse himself for a "refill" or bathroom break and returned only after Richard or Casie had moved on to greet other students.

After one such occasion, Micah returned to challenge Andrew to a table tennis match. "Where's Mei-Lien?"

"Over there." Andrew gestured with his head to the women sitting near the wall. "Why do you always take off?"

"I feel like Richard and Casie are baby-sitting. Every damn time Casie comes over, she drags off Mei-Lien."

"Well, maybe Mei-Lien wants to talk with Casie?"

"She's too polite to say no. Look at her. She keeps looking over at us."

"They're just trying to help us feel welcome. Give them a break."

"You asked."

~

One day as Andrew inched toward the cafeteria sandwich bar he noticed Mei-Lien getting into line. "I've never seen you here before," he said after moving to the back of the queue to stand with her.

"I usually go home for lunch with my parents. We only live a few blocks away. But they're both in meetings today, so I decided to eat here."

Over lunch Andrew discovered that Mei-Lien was born to Chinese immigrants who fled Mainland China during the height of Mao's cultural revolution. Her parents had been university professors in China and after a brief stint in Hong Kong, obtained asylum in the USA and jobs at the college. A couple years later they married.

"That's amazing! You must be so proud of them."

"Yes, yes, I am proud," said Mei-Lien softly, looking down.

Andrew's background was vapid in comparison. He'd lived his entire life in a small, suburban bungalow on a quiet street in a waning community.

Both ate in silence for a few moments while Andrew searched for topics to keep the conversation going. "How did you decide to become a doctor?"

"That's always been the plan since . . . I don't know when. Science comes easy to me. Must be in the genes. I'll be able to help people . . ." Then blushing, "My parents really want me to be a doctor as well. They're paying for my education . . . I mean, I have won some scholarships—not enough to cover everything, but my parents won't let me work. Education is very important to them."

Andrew's thoughts drifted to the day he'd left for college. His dad, a mailman, gave him a hug, ruffled his hair and then returned to the living room to his favourite easy chair. His mother, a secretary at the local school, drove Andrew to the bus depot, made sure his baggage was safely stowed, and cried as she watched the bus pull away. A care package arrived each month—all his parents could contribute to his education.

"Why do you want a BA in business?" asked Mei-Lien.

"More job opportunities when I graduate. And I was able to get a scholarship."

"And your parents? They're pleased?"

"Oh, yeah. They're happy I'm going to college. They would have been happy, too, if I wanted to be a plumber."

Mei-Lien looked up, "Really? Or are you joking?"

"No," said Andrew, puzzled that Mei-Lien would find this surprising. "As long as I'm honest, can pay my bills and enjoy my work, they don't care."

Andrew finished the last of his lunch and fiddled with his plastic knife. "You want to have lunch together another time? I mean, when you can?"

Mei-Lien stiffened. "My parents are pretty strict about . . . Medical school is really competitive . . . total focus on studies . . . no dating."

"It doesn't have to be a date. We can just eat together. I like talking to you."

"Okay," said Mei-Lien tentatively, "give me your phone number and I'll let you know the next time I'll be around."

CHAPTER 5

"So why don't you want to come home for lunch?" queried Mei-Lien's mother curtly as she opened the steamer, spooning out a bowl of rice for breakfast.

"I *never* came home for lunch in high school. What's the big deal now?"

"We have perfectly good food right here at home. And you want to eat that packaged . . . processed . . ." Mrs. Zhang hunted for the right word and eventually fell back on a common Chinese obscenity.

"It's not shit."

"Don't swear."

Mei-Lien closed her eyes and shifted her weight to one foot. Chinese profanity only became crude when translated.

"You and Dad eat with the other professors sometimes. Why can't I eat with my friends?"

"I don't want to see your grades drop."

"They won't."

Mei-Lien walked out the door. Elation at this small concession was squelched by her weariness with her parents' vigilance, with defending anything that appeared to diverge from the established regime. Her father staunchly upheld a total commitment to study. Her mother scrutinized the minutiae of her life and challenged the slightest impression that her academic goals were not preeminent.

Her mother was passionate about the ideals of her adopted nation but grumbled about the laziness of its young people and worried Mei-Lien might follow suit.

Mei-Lien forced back tears and twinges of resentment. She had never given her parents cause to worry. Hadn't she brought home academic awards? Scholarships for pre-med? Honours in her study of Chinese culture and languages—not only Mandarin but Cantonese as well? Mei-Lien thought during college her parents would relax their hold, after all, they lived just a few blocks from the campus. But proximity only tightened the reins. Surprisingly, her parents never objected to the monthly student gatherings.

~

"What's up?" asked Andrew as he slid his tray across from Mei-Lien and sat down.

"It's that obvious?" Mei-Lien closed the textbook she had attempted to read as she nibbled on her lunch.

"Try one of these strawberries, they look pretty good."

Mei-Lien reached for the fruit and ate it. Andrew smiled, enjoying her savour the strawberry. Then as spontaneous as her flush of affection and gratitude came the swell of anguish and tears.

"My God, Mei-Lien, is it that bad?"

Tears pouring down, Mei-Lien shook her head, now in the crook of her arm that rested on the table. Andrew gently stroked her hand. She entwined a couple of fingers in his and slowly the tears subsided. A few students passing nearby gave curious glances but there was no one else at their table and the noontime hubbub muffled Mei-Lien's quiet sobs.

Andrew had never seen Mei-Lien upset, occasionally subdued, but always with a ready smile, always willing to engage.

Gradually Mei-Lien quieted and pulled her head up but was too embarrassed to glance at Andrew.

"I'm so sorry," she whispered, "I don't . . . God, I must look a mess."

Andrew opened the bottle of water on Mei-Lien's tray and poured some out on a paper napkin. "Here, this will help."

Mei-Lien dabbed her face but still made no eye contact.

"What's going on?" asked Andrew gently.

"It's my mom . . . She gets to me sometimes . . . I mean . . . I get it . . . They suffered a lot. It wasn't just political. They're Catholic, intensely Catholic. If they'd stayed in China, they could have been imprisoned. They had to get out. So they fled, lost everything, left their families." Mei-Lien pulled out a tissue.

"But now that's all I hear . . . What they went through . . . How easy it is for me . . . I get so sick of it and then feel guilty. My mom's afraid I'm going to . . . I don't know, fall into some horrible abyss."

"Why would she think that?"

"I don't know. I've done everything they've ever asked me. There was only one time in junior high . . ."

"You jumped into a horrible abyss in junior high?"

Mei-Lien laughed in spite of herself and started to eat some of the cucumbers in her vegetable dish.

"I decided to Americanize my name and introduce myself as Emily."

"When you decide to defy, you really go big."

"Well, it may seem like nothing to you . . . So a friend calls up looking for Emily—something I hadn't calculated on—and a firestorm erupts . . . my mom spewing out a lecture on the ancient history and beauty of the Chinese culture. Emily! Did I think I could just discard a name given at birth? A name given in love? A strong and graceful name—beautiful lotus! My God, you'd think it was the end of the world. I backed off Emily."

Andrew started to laugh and Mei-Lien joined in, no longer shamed by her tear-stained eyes.

"It seems so funny telling you but I've never considered it humorous before—never told anyone, that's for sure."

"Am I too late?" said Micah, sitting next to Mei-Lien. Then noticing her splotched eyes said, "Hey, what happened?".

"Mother issues," said Andrew. "We're laughing about it now."

"When you move on to daddy issues, I have plenty to contribute."

"We're going to have to schedule another session," smirked Andrew. They went over their schedules to set up their next compatible lunch hour.

CHAPTER 6

Mrs. Zhang walked into what should have been the extra bedroom upstairs. The room had been converted into an office for her husband. Her office was in the den on the first floor. She stood near the window, peering down into the backyard. The temperatures were dropping but the afternoon sun warmed Mei-Lien as she studied at the patio table.

"I worry about Mei-Lien."

Mr. Zhang never acknowledged his wife until she spoke. It wasn't uncommon for her to wander in, gaze out the window and leave without a word.

"What's she done now?"

"She's changing."

~

Following two miscarriages, Mei-Lien was born healthy and beautiful. She grew to be a talented and lovely daughter, much admired by their friends. The Zhang home was peppered with framed photos taken through the years when Mrs. Zhang did not have these concerns; photos that captured milestones, moments of achievement and festivities. In her later teens Mrs. Zhang sensed a lessening of interest in family activities. During school breaks, Mei-Lien was not so eager to visit family friends on the East Coast. She preferred they all stay home or travel to other parts of the US. She wanted to get a job, earn her own money even though she had everything she needed. "When you're set up in a profession, you'll make money," Mrs. Zhang insisted. "Now is the time to study!"

~

"Mei-Lien will never know what we went through," said Mrs. Zhang to her husband. "She'll never really appreciate what she has."

"We've told her."

"Words! What are words?"

"What more could we have done? Chinese cultural school since she was in pre-school! She knows the history, the languages, the dance! She'll be taking her grade seven piano exams in the spring. "

"She's good at everything and brilliant in nothing."

As if conscious of being watched, Mei-Lien rose from her chair, stretched and walked onto the lawn. Mrs. Zhang pulled away from the window.

"She'll never know what it means to hide in fear during Mass, to pray with your heart beating, your ear attuned for any odd creak or footstep. She'll never watch her friends or neighbours get dragged away, never be torn from her family, never sent to labour camps," whispered Mrs. Zhang, bitter at the memories, frustrated that her daughter, though born from her womb, would never innately appreciate what they had suffered or sacrificed to give her life.

"Mei-Lien is soft, yes. But do you want *that* for her?"

"Stop being the lawyer," Mrs. Zhang snapped. "Mei-Lien is not afraid enough. She's too trusting. Trust makes you stupid."

"She's your daughter."

"Yours as well." It was a delicate topic. They had married late and Mr. Zhang hoped for a son. Both agreed on how they wanted their daughter raised but Mrs. Zhang considered the responsibility to be primarily her own.

CHAPTER 7

One day toward the middle of November, Richard met Andrew as he came out of class. "Do you have anything going on this Friday?"

"Working most likely. Why do you ask?"

"Christmas is coming up and we were planning an Advent Bible study." The invitation caught Andrew off-guard. He had enjoyed the camaraderie of their get-togethers but there had never been any suggestion of religious affiliation.

"Advent?" Andrew's dad was Catholic and his mother made sure, faithful to her promise at marriage, that Andrew was baptized, received First Communion, went to Confession, and was confirmed in the Catholic Church. They attended Mass on the major feast days and special occasions and . . . that was about it. If Andrew had heard of Advent, it hadn't made the least impression.

"Advent. It's the beginning of the liturgical year, prepares us for Christmas."

Liturgical year was still Greek to Andrew but preparing for Christmas was understandable. For a free meal, he would have been game to give it a try but he didn't want to ask if dinner was included. "I'll have to check my schedule."

"Have you enjoyed our other events?"

"Yeah . . . sure."

"Then, believe me, this will be even better." He handed Andrew a flyer from the FonS Student Association. "We'll be meeting at our centre just a couple blocks off campus."

As Richard walked off, Andrew looked over the flyer. Four Friday meetings, ending on the last day of class. *The group seems nice enough,* thought Andrew, *and they've given me plenty of meals. If I leave early I can still make my shift at work. Hell, why not. And I'll probably see Mei-Lien and Micah.*

~

Andrew tentatively opened the unlocked door of the FonS Student Association Centre and could hear voices coming from the rear of the converted home. He skirted past the sofas and chairs arranged in a circle and noted the piano with a guitar and djembe drums nearby. There was no longer a doubt regarding the Catholic connection. Crucifixes and icons of Jesus, Mary and the saints hung on every wall, even a Celtic cross in the bathroom, as he later discovered.

"Andrew, so glad you could make it," said Richard brightly as he noticed Andrew walking toward the dining/kitchen area.

"Sorry to be a little late. I had to finish off a paper this afternoon."

"No problem. We're just having a bite to eat before we begin. Come on in!"

Andrew stopped and looked at a painting of the FonS logo. The F and S were slanted outward with a bright sun over the <u>on</u> and a stream of water flowing beneath it.

"That's what we're all about," said Richard, following his gaze. "Christ is the sun and the fount of life. We are to lead others to him through friendship and service."

Andrew continued on to the dining area. As he served himself a bowl of chili, he noted Mei-Lien eating on the other side of the room and smiled a greeting. He glanced around for Micah, but he wasn't there. In fact, compared with the other events, the attendance was rather sparse.

"Where is everyone?" Andrew asked Richard.

"Oh, for some events we only invite those we think will appreciate the experience," Richard said kindly.

Andrew had no idea what could have distinguished him from those absent, but having arrived late, he had no time to pursue the thought. He wolfed down his chili and tucked a couple of buns into his pocket for his walk back to campus. He joined the group as they settled into the sofas and chairs he had passed earlier, clinching a seat next to Mei-Lien.

The music began immediately: a pulsing, vibrant tune. Before the singing began, Richard joined the piano and guitar on a djembe drum, beating out a spirited rhythm, agilely mirroring the tempo with his upper body. At intervals, he looked up, smiling broadly at the group that encircled him. Casie, his assistant at all the events, offered drums to the newcomers, encouraging them to join in. When the drums had been passed out, Richard and Casie broke into song. The refrain was repetitive and easy to learn. Soon most of the group were singing along, some with their eyes closed, hands raised, swaying from side to side. A priest quietly entered the room and sat in a chair reserved for him.

After a prayer and scripture reading, Fr. Raymond, as he was introduced, sat forward on his chair, rested his elbows on his knees, and brought his fingertips together.

"Have you ever considered why you are here?" He looked around at the students. "Why study? Why work? Why pray? What is your purpose? Have you ever considered your true purpose?" The priest paused and lowered his head as though deep in thought. "And the next question comes spontaneously. How do we know our purpose? We are all here for a reason. God has a plan for us all. Outside of that plan, we will never be happy. So the most important quest in life is to discover God's will for our lives.

"Isn't that the message of the scriptures today? If Mary had not followed God's will, Jesus would never have been born. Our salvation would never have come to pass. So what about you, and you, and you?" The priest pointed to various students in the room. "What will be your response? Do you want to waste your life outside of God's will? Or do you have the courage to discover God's purpose for your life and follow it to the end?"

The priest paused for several minutes. "How do you know God's will for your life? The devil is sly and can convince us to follow our own whims. God, however, provides us with his representatives to lead us in his way."

Andrew nudged Mei-Lien, "Representatives?"

"You have a question?" asked Fr. Raymond. "You don't need to whisper."

"Well . . ." said Andrew, "Who are these representatives of God?"

"Spiritual guides who have been trained to distinguish what comes from God and what comes from the devil, such as myself," said Fr. Raymond, "We are key to helping people understand God's will for their lives. Next week we'll talk more about discovering God's will."

Richard said, "Let us pray." He spread open his arms, closed his eyes and prayed that all those present today would have the boldness to seek God's will and the fortitude to follow it.

Another rousing song began but Andrew was out the door before the drums joined in, sprinting to work without having had a chance to chat with Mei-Lien.

~

"So you skipped out on the Bible study," said Andrew when he saw Micah the next week.

"What Bible study?"

"Richard didn't give you a flyer?"

"No, I didn't get a flyer." Micah started laughing. "I knew there had to be a catch."

"He probably couldn't find you."

"Who cares!" said Micah, still laughing. "So who's the group? The Mormons? Evangelicals?"

"They're Catholic."

"Oh, so the Catholics are at it now! These religions must share the same game plan. Well, the food was great while it lasted. See you later, gotta go." Micah was still grinning and shaking his head as he walked down the hall.

Exams, final papers, and his job at the bookstore overruled any consideration of further Bible studies. Richard continued to meet Andrew in the hallways and encourage him to attend. "You give a couple hours to God and God will inspire you a hundredfold with your school work." But Andrew fell back on the adage of his mother: "God helps those who help themselves" and skipped the Bible studies.

CHAPTER 8

Andrew stepped off his bed and admired the scroll—Mei-Lien's Christmas gift. The long, narrow paper had several lines of Chinese characters that were as captivating in their beauty as they were mysterious in their intent. On the back, in a corner, Mei-Lien had written, *"A bit of fragrance clings to the hand that gives flowers."* Looking at the scroll brought back his last rendezvous with Mei-Lien before the Christmas break.

~

They had just finished their lunch together and were sitting on a bench in a corner of a campus green space. Andrew pulled a gift from his backpack and handed it to Mei-Lien.

"You didn't have to get me a gift!" she said. But the brightness in her voice showed she was touched that he had thought of her. As she carefully peeled back the tape, Andrew began to doubt his choice. He had had no idea what to give Mei-Lien and scanned the shelves of the college bookstore until he had settled on a knitted scarf and hat in the college colours. It was utterly mundane; she would think it was stupid. Yet as soon as she folded back the wrapping, Mei-Lien had donned his gift and playfully wrapped the scarf around their necks.

"And I have something for you!" said Mei-Lien. Out of her bag she pulled a long, slender box, carefully wrapped. When Andrew started to peel off the tape, Mei-Lien said, "No, no. Not here. When you are back in your room, open the gift and remember me." She stood up, "I have to go. My parents are expecting me." Then she opened her arms for a hug.

Andrew had expected a brief, pat-on-the-back squeeze. Instead, Mei-Lien nestled her chin on Andrew's chest and held him tight as Andrew wrapped her in his arms. They stayed there, gently rocking until Mei-Lien said, "I'll miss you." Both pulled back hesitantly, and without thinking, Andrew gently pressed his lips to Mei-Lien's. Mei-Lien responded with a long, lingering kiss. Neither said a word as they pulled back and Mei-Lien walked away. Andrew watched her go. Right before she passed out of sight she turned and waved. With a spring in his step, Andrew turned and strolled back to his dorm.

CHAPTER 9

The over-arching branches of the ancient trees screened the day's remaining light, casting shadows on the chipped, uneven sidewalk. In the windows of several homes Christmas trees glittered with coloured lights. Every so often Micah squinted through the growing dusk to make out the house number. As he approached a crossroad, a faded "No Exit" sign warned of an upcoming dead-end. Micah paused. *If it's not on this block . . .* He tapped his pants pocket with the last of his cash and continued down the street.

He knew he was taking a chance, coming to Andrew's place unannounced, but he had to get out of his house: relatives camped in every corner and spilling into an RV parked in the driveway; his cousins, uncles and father and their unending desire to play football; his father, unable to understand Micah's disinterest, constantly urging him to get off his butt and play. He was sick of it. With little more money than the cost of a round-trip bus ticket, Micah told his family he was going to visit a friend.

The last house on the right was Andrew's. Micah walked to the barricade with the huge "Dead End" sign and looked beyond. A ravine dropped precariously, its depth hidden in the shadows of dusk. The meandering chasm divided the residential neighbourhood from what appeared to be an industrial area on the other side. Micah leaned against the barricade. Andrew's home, like those around it, was a small, dated bungalow surrounded by trimmed shrubs. A sedan was parked on the gravel driveway that ran from the curb and stopped at the side of the house. There was no porch, just a long over-hang that covered the couple of steps leading to the front door. As Micah walked closer to the house he noticed the faded paint and the weatherworn door. Not only was his visit unexpected, he thought, it would most likely be an imposition. *Well, even if it's for one night, I have nowhere else to go.* Micah rang the bell.

~

"Micah?" exclaimed Andrew when he opened the door. Both Andrew and Micah had exchanged phone numbers and addresses weeks ago but neither had expected to see the other until after the Christmas break.

"Come on in!" said Andrew as he gave Micah a hug. "Great to see you! Have a seat." Micah went for the recliner. "Just not that one . . . My dad's in the shower and that's his next stop. I'll get my mom."

Micah dropped his backpack and settled on the couch that backed into the front window. From where he sat, Micah watched Andrew pass through the dining room and open the kitchen door. In moments, a middle-aged woman came through the door drying her hands on a dishtowel. Her short hair was blown back with a casual, yet stylish air. As they entered the living room, Andrew's mom said, "I hear a friend of Andrew's has come to visit."

Andrew, following close behind, introduced them.

"Wonderful to meet you," she said as she gave Micah a gentle hug. "Just call me Sonia. And, of course, you'll have dinner with us, won't you?"

"Yes, thanks . . . if it's not inconvenient."

"No problem at all. So good of you to come. Andrew has told us a lot about you. Do you have a place to stay for the night?"

Micah glanced at Andrew.

"You're more than welcome to stay with us," said Sonia. "Andrew, why don't you let Micah have your bed. When your brother arrives, you two can decide who will sleep on the pull-out couch." Sonia turned back toward the kitchen, "You boys get settled in and I'll finish supper." Pausing at the kitchen door, she turned and said, "And, *change the sheets!*"

Andrew grabbed Micah's backpack and led him into the dining room. Midway to the right was a door that led to a short, narrow hallway.

"The bathroom," said Andrew, pointing to the door ahead of them as they entered the hallway. "My parents' bedroom is at the front of the house and my brother and I share a bedroom in the back . . . or shared. We're hardly here anymore. He's coming home in a couple of days."

Just then the front bedroom door opened. "Now who's this?" said an affable man in a fresh cotton shirt and jeans, combing back his wet, greying hair with his fingers.

"Micah, this is my dad."

"Call me Keith," said Andrew's dad as he and Micah shook hands. "Go ahead now and make that bed before your mother gets after you."

"I hear you, Keith!" hollered Sonia from the kitchen.

"No secrets in this house," winked Keith as he walked toward the living room.

"I can still hear you, Keith!" shouted back Sonia.

Micah and Andrew entered the rear bedroom. It was just large enough for two single beds with a dresser in between. Andrew tossed Micah's backpack near one of the beds. "That'll be your bed."

"Sorry I didn't call before . . . I don't know what I was thinking. I can sleep on the couch."

"Hey, man. I'm happy you came. You heard my parents: they love having my friends over."

"When everyone is over for Christmas, it gets a little crazy at my place," said Micah as he and Andrew stripped and made the beds. "This year, it got to be too much." Micah shook a pillow into a clean pillowcase. "Don't you have relatives visiting for Christmas?"

"No. My dad was an only child. Not long after I was born, his parents both died in a car accident."

"Shit!"

"Yeah . . . my dad had a breakdown around that time."

"What! Why didn't you ever tell me this?"

"He's okay now . . . Mom says he became more subdued. He delivers mail and then he's home. My mom's family is in the Midwest. She came to California for a summer job and met my dad. We usually see her side of the family in the summer."

"Boys!" Sonia called out from the dining room, "It's time to eat."

~

The meal was almost finished when the front door swung open and a tall, lanky man strode into the dining room.

"Ra-pha-el Co-vick!" said Sonia, emphasizing every syllable. "We weren't expecting you until the twenty-ninth!" She was up in a flash, embracing her eldest son. The dining area became crowded with family members up, sliding behind chairs, embracing. Micah was introduced and hugged like a member of the family. Raph, as he was called, was soon seated at the table with a plate and utensils and proceeded to finish off the left-overs of the Christmas turkey dinner that Sonia had warmed for their supper.

"So, the college boy is back at last! How's it going?" asked Raph.

Andrew and Micah related some experiences, concluding with their exams and final papers.

"Glad that's behind me," said Raph.

"What did you study?" asked Micah.

"Liberal Arts with a minor in Fine Arts." Raph took an apple from the fruit bowl. "I want to get into the film scene. We'll see how it goes. Found a job helping to construct sets. It's a start."

"You're good with your hands, Raph. During high school you always had something creative going on in woodworking class," said Keith.

Turning toward Andrew and Micah, Sonia asked, "Do you boys have plans for the next few days?"

"How long can you stay, Micah?" asked Andrew.

"Well . . . really . . . I hadn't thought . . . I have to be back home by the thirty-first—my mom's side of the family is planning something for New Years."

"Hey, Andrew," said Raph, "that gives us a few days to show Micah around the town."

"Enjoy yourselves," said Keith, "I'm going to watch some TV."

Sonia stood up and began gathering dishes and her sons joined in. Micah followed them into the small back kitchen where they set to work washing the dishes and cleaning the counters. Sonia tossed a dishcloth to Micah. "Would you give the table a wipe?"

As the tasks were finishing, Sonia pulled out a bottle of wine and a glass. "I'm having Zinfandel. Bring a glass to the dining room if you'd like some. Otherwise, there's beer in the fridge. Andrew, would you bring a beer to your dad?"

With drinks in hand, sitting around the dining room table, Raph talked about his experiences in LA which morphed into old family stories, politics, best movies they'd seen, and on and on. Keith passed through on his way to bed, getting ready for an early workday, and the conversation rolled on. It was after midnight when Sonia left the three young men as they made plans for the next few days.

CHAPTER 10

"This must be *some* restaurant," said Andrew. "It's taken us an hour to get here."

"You can be the judge," said Raph as his hatchback rolled to a stop and he opened his door.

It was Micah's last day. His bus left the bus depot in a few hours.

Micah and Andrew stepped out onto the sidewalk and took in the large Victorian home. It was set back some distance from the curb with a broad lawn on either side of the house.

"Come on. I'll give you a tour," said Raph. "It's a bed and breakfast."

He led them across the front lawn past flowerbeds of succulents to the rear of the house with its spacious and beautifully landscaped backyard. The sides of the property and the entire backyard were enclosed by tall evergreen shrubs and shaded by oak and palm trees. There were more than a dozen people already enjoying morning brunch on the veranda and in the patio.

"How did you find this place?" asked Andrew.

"Friends. The restaurant is open for brunch and supper. There are four or five rooms available for overnight guests."

They walked up the steps to the veranda and passed through a screen door to the back of the house. There were a few tables inside but only one was occupied. A long, antique credenza served as a counter that separated the dining area from the kitchen beyond. Against one sidewall was a narrow table that bore granola, fruit, pastries and other breakfast foods. Above this table, in coloured chalk, was written the hot breakfast options of the day.

"Hey, Raph!" said the middle-aged man behind the counter. "We were just talking about you. How are you doing?"

Raph chatted briefly about his work in LA. Then turning to Andrew and Micah he said, "Choose whatever you like. Brunch is on me."

With their orders placed, the young men found a table on the veranda.

It wasn't long before their plates were served. "Andrew, Micah," said Raph, "I want you to meet Jeff," indicating the man who had just served their orders. "He's the manager of the B&B and also runs the kitchen."

Jeff shook hands with Andrew and Micah as they exchanged greetings and introductions. He remained at the table for a few minutes bantering with Raph about bed bugs and burnt toast. Andrew, Micah and customers at nearby tables laughed and added an occasional rejoinder.

"What a guy!" said Raph after Jeff left to return to the kitchen.

"Do you come here often?" asked Andrew. "It looks like you know each other really well."

"We're close friends. I come here as often as I can."

"He seems like a great guy," added Micah, exchanging a significant glance with Raph.

"Yeah, he is."

Raph and Andrew dropped Micah off at the bus depot and were heading home.

"Gotta say, you know how to pick out friends," said Raph. "Micah's a decent guy."

"Yeah, about that . . . Your friend is pretty decent as well. Jeff? That was his name, right?"

"He's the best."

"What was the name of the bed and breakfast? I didn't notice any sign."

"Sure there was, near the menu, *Bread and Berth.* Get it: B&B."

"There was no sign outside."

"No need. The B&B gets enough business from referrals."

Andrew looked out the window at the rolling hills, tinged with green after the recent rains. He recalled the obvious affection between Jeff and Raph, the knowing looks exchanged between Raph and Micah, and the predominantly male clientele at the B&B.

"Are you gay?" asked Andrew.

"Would that be a problem for you?"

"So Micah's gay, too," concluded Andrew.

"His family doesn't know."

"Does Mom know . . . about you?"

"Mom's known for years; Dad, a couple of years ago."

"Why didn't you tell me?"

"I assumed you'd figure it out for yourself."

"Yeah, at a gay B&B with my best friend. And Jeff, I take it, is your partner?"

"You always were a little slow on the uptake," said Raph good-naturedly, trying to lighten the growing tension. But Andrew would not be assuaged.

"Why do you always treat me like a kid? You and Mom. Your big discussions in the kitchen, always sending me away with, 'Why don't you go play a game of cards with your dad.'"

"Andrew, give me a break. I left for college when you were twelve. You had Mom all to yourself."

"And when you came home, I'd be shooed out again, even as a teenager."

"Only when I had things I wanted to talk to Mom about . . . alone."

"Yeah, I can see that now. Raph, I'm not six years old, get that through your head. And you would never have brought me to your exclusive B&B if Micah had not been here."

"We brought you to the B&B so you could figure it out," entreated Raph.

"Why didn't you just tell me?"

"Andrew . . ."

"Shut up. I don't want to talk about it anymore."

~

A longstanding, unacknowledged resentment which simmered in Andrew came spewing to the surface: years of being pushed out of conversations, sent out to play, told to join his dad in the living room. "Let them solve the problems of the world and we'll enjoy ourselves," his dad would say when they heard bits of the animated discussions coming from the kitchen.

As he grew older, Andrew wanted to be part of the discussions between his mom and Raph, but felt guilty leaving his dad alone. At times, even now, he felt he was still treated like a kid who couldn't handle serious subjects. As these sentiments gushed to the surface, he was ashamed to realize that he was jealous of his witty and engaging brother who was unafraid to spout off his opinions and got his mother to laugh. His seething emotions threatened the love and admiration he'd always had for Raph.

CHAPTER 11

Andrew had had a couple of conversations with his mother and Raph and a few days to reflect on his reaction to his brother in the car. Sonia agreed with Andrew: if Raph and Micah were ready to share that they were gay, they should have told Andrew before bringing him to the B&B and introducing him to Raph's partner. On the other hand, she had always respected Raph's decisions as to when and to whom he shared this personal information and Andrew would have to accept that Raph had not been ready to tell him until now.

~

While unassuming in demeanour, Sonia was uncanny in perception. Dealing with her husband's breakdown and stint in a mental institution had given Sonia a profound empathy for persons who, from the sidelines, peer through a societal glass wall into the realm of presumed normality. The experience had made her receptive to her bewildered and anxious son when, at seventeen, he shared his growing homosexual feelings. And through her research and conversations at home, she had paved the way for her husband and Andrew to accept Raph when, in his own time, he decided to open up to them.

~

One evening when Andrew and his mom were alone, she appealed to him further: could he not fathom that Raph wouldn't want to risk confusing and losing the love of a younger brother by sharing information he wasn't ready to handle? And when it came to Andrew remaining with his father instead of joining in the discussions between her and Raph, she almost laughed. Did it ever cross his mind that his father played cards with him because he thought Andrew wasn't interested in joining in the conversations? Since his breakdown, Keith did not enjoy discussions about politics or issues that left him feeling helpless or angry. He knew his limits. He enjoyed playing cards with Andrew but would have also been content to watch a TV program or read a book. Did Andrew think that she would have consistently excluded her husband from any conversation? Andrew's mind and emotions churned with shifting perspectives and left him feeling stripped and humbled.

CHAPTER 12

Andrew sat at a back table in the cafeteria sipping hot chocolate and looking over the course selection for the winter semester.

"Welcome back. Mind if I join you?"

Andrew glanced up as Micah took off his jacket. "No," he said as he continued to pore over the course catalogue.

"I thought you had already registered for your courses."

"I did. But the time of one course has been changed so now I have a conflict. I need to choose another literature course." Andrew flipped the page and scanned his options while Micah watched from the other side of the table.

"Raph called and told me about . . ."

"I figured he would."

"Are you okay with . . ." Micah looked over his shoulder.

"Why didn't you just tell me you were gay?" Andrew asked, perplexed.

"Would you keep your voice down?" said Micah, leaning in closer. "I would have if I'd known your brother was gay."

"Yeah, and you found that out before me," said Andrew, deflated.

"Look at it from my side," said Micah, whispering. "If my parents find out, I don't know how they'll take it. My dad will be disgusted . . . You should hear his comments about 'fags.' It's hard to know whom to tell, when to tell. I didn't want to lose you as a friend. And Mei-Lien?

Can you imagine what would happen if *her* parents found out?"

"Are you going to tell her?"

"Probably not . . . not any time soon."

Andrew flipped a couple more pages absently. "You should tell Mei-Lien. She's not her mom."

"It's scary. People don't treat you the same. Guys I know got beat up pretty bad when they came out."

"Look—I don't care that you and Raph are gay, okay? I just wish you would have told me."

"And we're still friends?"

"Of course."

Micah jumped over to the table and sat next to Andrew, pulling the catalogue between them. "Find anything interesting?"

"Kind of intrigued by this course," said Andrew, pointing out the listing.

Micah leaned in to see, "Who teaches it?"

"Rev. Hachette."

"I'm registered for the course! Sign up. We can take it together."

CHAPTER 13

"Where have you been hiding?" asked Andrew as he slid next to Mei-Lien in the cafeteria.

"We just got in last night. I was hoping to be back for at least part of the Christmas break, but my parents' invitation in New York was extended. It seems the Chinese government is becoming more open towards the Catholic Church. My parents and their friends think it's a trap, some kind of sellout. My God, four weeks of endless meetings, talks, dinners, Masses—and me cramped in the same hotel room as my parents the whole time. Ugh!" Mei-Lien put her elbow on the table, dropped her chin on her palm and crossed her eyes.

"What do they mean by a sellout?" asked Andrew.

"Who knows. It actually sounded like a good thing to me. I just sat in a corner, read a book and tried to block out the endless discussions. What's up with you?"

Andrew considered telling Mei-Lien about his break, but thought the better of it. "I took on an extra course this semester. It's going to be tight with work and all. Why don't we study together sometimes?" said Andrew.

"Like my mom's going to let that happen."

"There are study rooms in the library we can sign out. Micah will join us when he can. At least we can get together more often."

~

Micah slipped into the library study room and plopped his backpack on the floor. "Hard at it already," he said as he pulled out an opened package of red licorice from his jacket pocket and offered it to Andrew and Mei-Lien. "Snacks are on me today."

"Hey, thanks," said Mei-Lien as she took out a couple of ropes.

"Yeah, thanks, man," said Andrew.

As Micah rummaged through his backpack for his schedule he said, "When I came in, I saw your mom in the history section over there," gesturing to the right with his chin.

"Oh, shit!" said Mei-Lien, slamming closed her day planner and gathering her notebooks.

Micah laughed. "I take it she still doesn't know about our plan to study together."

"And I take it my mom is not here," said Mei-Lien.

Micah and Andrew bent over in laughter. Mei-Lien got up and pounded Micah on his shoulders and back with her notebook. "You! I'll get you back. You just wait and see!" Then turning to Andrew she began to whack him as well. "Yeah, you, too. Just wait."

"Well, Micah got your heart pumping," said Andrew. "Won't be falling asleep anytime soon." Andrew gave Micah a high-five while Mei-Lien sat back down and opened up her books.

"Just you wait," she said as she reopened her day planner. "Are we going to set up some study dates . . . now that Micah has arrived?" She took another rope of licorice and playfully wacked him with it.

After the dates had been set and they began to pack up, Andrew said, "The college is sponsoring a Super Bowl event. Setting up a monitor in the student centre . . . pots of chili, pizza."

"I didn't know you were interested in football," said Micah.

"I'm not."

Micah looked over, surprised. Mei-Lien smiled, "The ads, right?"

"Yeah, how did you know?"

"My dad's into football. Super Bowl is his big thing. My mom hates it."

"Does your mom like anything?" asked Micah.

"Yes, Chinese opera." Mei-Lien made a face. "It can shatter glass. Thank God, my dad is no fan. One of my parents' few divided fronts, so I don't have to go to any performances."

"Are you going to the Super Bowl on campus?"

"Not me," said Mei-Lien. "I can watch all the ads at home with an endless supply of spring rolls and dim sum."

"Maybe I'll drop by your place," said Micah.

"Nice try," said Mei-Lien as she walked off.

CHAPTER 14

Andrew slid into a desk near Micah moments before Fr. Fred Hachette walked through the door—rather, charged through the door, his head bent forward of his long, lanky legs. *The Mad Hatter!* Fr. Hachette dropped his worn leather satchel on the desk and shot frequent glances at the students as he rummaged through its contents, finally pulling out a sheaf of papers.

"So how the hell is everyone? Bloody damp out there."

Some students smiled, amused. Others widened their eyes and gave knowing glances to friends. Andrew turned to Micah with a look of amazement.

"The name's Hachette, Fred Hachette, Rev. Hachette, Fred: your preference. How many of you came prepared with Graham Greene?"

Most raised their hands. "Good. For those of you who haven't, there'll be no pampering in this class. Buy, borrow, smuggle—I don't give a damn. Just come to this class prepared. Every title we'll read is readily available; however, if you are looking for a copy at midnight before the class, you may run into problems. Go over the book list today if you haven't already consulted your syllabus." Hachette raised the papers he held, gave them a shake, and then tossed them to the corner of the desk.

"This isn't a course for cop-outs or easy marks," said Hachette as he continued to rake through his satchel. "If you thought you could sail by, reading commentaries and synopses instead of doing your own thinking, leave now." He stopped digging through his bag and looked directly at the class. "I mean it. Leave now. I'm not interested in regurgitation."

Two students, to the side of Andrew, kept their heads down, busy taking notes, of what, Andrew couldn't begin to imagine.

"How many of you are familiar with Graham Greene?"

Several hands rose. Hachette nodded toward one.

"Dances with Wolves," the student replied.

"Not the actor." Hachette nodded to another who had raised her hand.

"The Power and the Glory."

"Good. Have you read it?"

"On the syllabus." The class laughed.

"Fair enough," Hachette chuckled. "This is your first class and the only class that you will attend without having first read the material and been prepared for discussion. And so in this session I give some background on the authors we'll be studying."

After class as they left the classroom building, Andrew and Micah saw Hachette leaning on a tree, cigarette between his fingers, smoke issuing from his nose.

"He's not half-bad," remarked Andrew.

"He's great."

"I've heard him called the Mad Hatter."

"Never heard that one," said Micah. "Most of students call him Puff, the Magic Dragon."

CHAPTER 15

Hachette strode into the classroom and dropped his satchel on the desk. "Let's see . . . here's the class list," he said as he drew out a folder. "Why don't we put some names to faces and see if I scared off anyone last week."

As he called the names, he sized up his class. There was his avid cohort, students who signed up for as many of his literature courses as their majors allowed. They stretched the rest of class with their perspectives and questions during discussions.

The let's-give-it-a-chance group made up the majority of his class. They took a course, learned quickly that high school book reports wouldn't pass muster, and grew in their engagement during discussions.

There were always a few who dawdled through with drooping lids. They slipped into the back desks and kept their eyes down, hoping to mask their lack of preparation.

And what would his class be without members of the Proclaimers of Christ who took his class with no further purpose than to report his crusty language and provocative statements to the dean of academics, the president of the college, or the bishop himself. The PoCs, as they were called, spent most of the class bent over their notebooks, feverously taking notes of anything and everything in the hopes of one day having him ousted. Sweet Jesus.

And lastly, there were those whose diploma or degree required a literature course and they happened to stumble into his lair because it suited their schedule. They were the wild cards. Fred loved watching their interest grow and their participation deepen . . . or not.

"Andrew Covik." Andrew gave a slight wave. "Ah, yes. I've seen you at the bookshop. What's your major?"

"Business."

Bingo. A wild card.

CHAPTER 16

Cheers and laughter hurtled through the foyer and enveloped
Andrew as he entered the student centre. The Super Bowl party
filled the spacious lobby. Students watched in chairs or sat on the
floor in front of the large monitor that projected the game. A waft of
savoury spices enticed Andrew to diminishing crock-pots of chili and
picked over trays of pizza. As he served up, a friendly hand grasped his
shoulder.

"I haven't seen you for awhile."

Andrew picked up a spoon and turned to see Richard. "Hi. . . yeah
. . . I've taken on more courses this semester and, with a job as well, I
don't have as much time as I did last semester." Andrew took a bite of
his chili. "This is great. You want to try some?"

"I already ate."

"If I had come any later I would have missed out completely. Had to
finish up some assignments. Hachette doesn't tolerate the unprepared."

Richard became grave and dropped his hand. "Fr. Fred Hachette?"

"That's the one," said Andrew spooning up more chili.

"You've met Fr. Raymond, right?"

"Was he the priest at the Bible study?"

"Yes, so you are familiar with him. He's the spiritual advisor of the
FonS Student Association. A fervent priest, very knowledgeable."

A roar of laughter exploded and Andrew knew he had missed a

commercial. "That's nice," he said as he edged backwards toward the chairs. *What do I care about Fr. Raymond.*

"Fr. Raymond has some serious concerns about Fr. Hachette's classes."

"He shouldn't. The guy's great."

"You should discuss this with Fr. Raymond."

"Why?" asked Andrew, irritation clenching his grip on the spoon and creeping into his voice.

"Because you shouldn't allow anyone to endanger your faith."

"Endanger my faith? What are you talking about?"

Laughter again resounded in the room. Andrew shot a glance toward the monitor. He had come primarily to enjoy the commercials and another had just scored without him.

Richard was oblivious to the jocularity of the students and Andrew's desire to join them. "Those of us at FonS take our education very seriously. We're not here to lose time with the frivolous or the erroneous and Hachette falls into both categories."

"Huh? Have you been to his classes?"

"I've heard enough about them."

"So you haven't taken any of his courses?"

Richard darted a glance at Andrew. "Others have and after hearing their concerns, Fr. Raymond decided that it would be best to avoid Hachette."

"The guy's fantastic." Andrew turned to end the conversation and find a seat.

"Go talk to Fr. Raymond," said Richard before he turned away.

The commercial break had just finished as Andrew sat down. *What the hell was that all about?* Andrew ate his chili and looked around. The cheers and jesting only bristled his confusion and simmering anger. *I don't have to answer to Richard. So I don't show up at their gigs, so what? I only wanted to meet up with Micah and Mei-Lien anyway. And now he's telling me to drop out of Hachette's class? Are you kidding me?*

"Hey, man, when was your last meal?" said the guy next to Andrew, watching him rapidly chomp through his chili. "I'll save your place while you get a refill. Looks like you're ready to eat the plate."

"It's that obvious?" quipped Andrew as he refocused on the people surrounding him. "Yeah, maybe I'll go for the last of the pizza."

~

Micah listened as Andrew recounted his conversation with Richard.

"I'm not surprised. Reminds me of high school."

"High school?"

"Oh, yeah. I went to a big school in the center of town and these good-looking college kids would come to volunteer and run activities. Everybody nice, nice, fun, fun. Then you'd get invited to a Bible study. After a while if you didn't show up for the religious stuff, you were disregarded. Not so nice, nice anymore." Micah shook his head, "I never liked Richard but I really thought the get-togethers were just part of a freshmen initiation—no strings attached."

"I feel bad for Mei-Lien. It's practically the only thing her parents allow her to do."

"No surprise there."

"What do you mean?"

"Now we know why Mei-Lien was able to go in the first place. Her parents probably knew the get-togethers were organized by the FonS gang. Unreal."

"Well, I don't expect I'll be getting any more invites."

"Mine stopped coming last term," smirked Micah. "They had me sorted out way before you—I'm so transparent."

Andrew gave him a shove and they walked off together laughing.

CHAPTER 17

"You take them too seriously." Mei-Lien snuggled closer to Andrew. Micah hadn't come to this study period. When he wasn't there or left early, Mei-Lien and Andrew studied cross-legged on the floor of the study room, their books spread out before them. It started simply enough when the outlay of notepads and reference books exceeded the table and they transferred everything to the floor. Then the jostling playfully as they packed up their materials shifted into lingering embraces. Now their sessions never ended without the books pushed aside and the two cuddling in the corner, sharing confidences.

"I'm telling you, there's something off with that group."

"You're just not used to going to church. At the FonS meetings we have something to eat, read from the Bible, talk about it, sing, and go home. Casie always asks about my studies."

"Why do you go at all?"

"It's about the only thing I can go to. Besides, I've made some friends . . . I met you." Mei-Lien turned upwards and kissed Andrew. "And Micah. And now sometimes I can go to church here on campus without travelling forty-five minutes to a Chinese Catholic Church with my parents."

"Do you want to go to church?" Andrew asked gently.

Mei-Lien sighed. "You'll laugh if I tell you."

Andrew kissed her forehead, "Trust me."

Mei-Lien played with a strand of her hair. "During high school I got so depressed," she said softly. "My parents were on me to keep up my grades and to excel in Chinese and in piano. I felt swallowed up. Then I went to a special teen Mass. There were some prayers and adoration afterward and . . . I felt a peace come over me . . . like it would be okay and I just sat there and wept. I believed it was God."

Andrew tightened his embrace.

"Not that that happens often. At times I feel like crying during a hymn . . . I do believe in God." There was silence between them for a few minutes. Then, as if an afterthought, "Sometimes Fr. Hachette says Mass in the campus chapel."

CHAPTER 18

Andrew sat on "their" bench, as he and Mei-Lien now called it. It was Sunday morning and the campus green space was quiet. Mei-Lien had permission to go to Mass on campus rather than with her parents. And now Andrew waited to bring her to breakfast at the cafeteria. It wasn't an ordinary breakfast. His entire family had come for a weekend visit, the first visit since he had arrived last fall. His parents, Raph and Jeff had arrived the evening before and taken Andrew out to dinner. This morning they were having breakfast in the campus cafeteria so they could meet Mei-Lien and reconnect with Micah.

"Boo!" Mei-Lien had come up behind him without Andrew noticing.

Andrew startled, then jumped over the bench and gave Mei-Lien a hug.

"I'm really looking forward to meeting your family!" said Mei-Lien. "I'm not late, am I?"

"No, not at all. Before you meet them though, I want to tell you something."

They both sat down on the bench. "My brother drove up with my parents," Andrew began.

"Yeah, you told me he would."

"He came with his partner." Mei-Lien looked at Andrew quizzically. "He's gay, Mei-Lien."

Nothing registered on Mei-Lien's face as she processed this information.

"Wow. I've never met anyone who was gay," said Mei-Lien thoughtfully.

"You probably have and just didn't know it."

Andrew and Mei-Lien sat quietly for a few minutes. "I haven't really thought much about homosexuality," said Mei-Lien. "When news reports of the gay parade in San Francisco are on TV, my parents are disgusted but we never talk about it. Homosexuality has never been a big concern for me—actually, it's never been *any* concern to me or anyone connected to me."

"You like Micah, right?"

"He's our friend, Andrew! Of course I like—"

Andrew watched as the realization washed over Mei-Lien.

"Yeah, he's gay," said Andrew.

"He's so normal . . ."

Andrew waited a few moments. "Do you still want to meet my family?" he asked softly.

Mei-Lien tucked her arm through Andrew's and smiled. "Let's go."

~

The conversation during breakfast was light and casual. Andrew and Micah teased Keith about his love of the "Golden Girls" TV program.

"I have to educate myself on how women age so I can deal with your mother when she gets older," quipped Keith.

Jeff poked fun at the cafeteria food and invited them all for brunch at his B&B. Mei-Lien's initial shyness faded away and she chatted about her courses with Andrew's mom, Sonia, who sat next to her.

They had long since finished their meal and were sipping the last of their coffee when Mei-Lien said, "I'd better be going."

"And we'd better get started on our tour," said Keith. "As much as this cafeteria is captivating, I'm sure there's more to see.

As they all stood to leave, Andrew noticed Casie eating with a small group of students. She was seated a few tables away observing all that passed at their table. When he caught her eye, she did not avert them until he smiled and winked. Then he turned and left with his family.

CHAPTER 19

"Short story this week," said Hachette. "I'm going easy before the finals." Some students laughed. "Graham Greene, 'A Visit with Morin'. Okay. Let's start with quotable quotes. Anyone?"

"Talking about Morin's writings: 'Where we did not understand his meaning, there were no editor's notes to kill speculation.'"

"Yes," said Hachette, "Remember that when you teach."

"I'll never be a teacher," said the student.

"We're all teachers. Now, any more quotes?"

"I've got a good one: 'Orthodox critics seemed to scent heresy like a rat dead somewhere under the boards, at a spot they could not locate.'"

There were a few chuckles.

"Listen to this," said another, "Morin describing the penny catechism: 'Questions and answers, smug and explanatory—mystery like a butterfly killed by cyanide, stiffened and laid out with pins and paper-strips.'"

A few students clapped and the student who had read the quote stood and bowed.

"Sit down," said Hachette with a smile. "Any more contributions?"

Andrew raised his hand tentatively and Hachette nodded in his direction.

"Dunlop, you know, the wine dealer who had read Morin's books as a student . . . Well, Dunlop drives home with Morin after midnight

Mass," said Andrew. "When they get to Morin's home, Dunlop asks Morin why he had left his front door open while he was at Mass. Morin tells him that several years before on Christmas Eve, a man froze to death on a doorstep because no one was home. Everyone was at church for midnight Mass. Morin seems so compassionate. I doubt anyone else left their door open. Yet later in the story Morin gets all tangled up in guilt over breaking precepts and regulations. I don't get it."

Hachette regarded Andrew momentarily then smiled at the class. "And so we begin."

~

Hachette slid a couple of books across the bookstore counter. "So are you off to an exotic location after exams?" he asked Andrew who was at the cash register.

"No, it's better!" Andrew said with a grin. "I plan to make a few extra bucks and take a couple of courses during the spring semester. I want to finish in three years if I can. Then I can think of exotic vacation spots."

"You set off a spirited discussion in our last class," said Hachette as he pulled out his wallet.

"Yeah, well, I'm still not so sure of Morin's position. On the one hand, I admire the guy and on the other . . . it's like he can't trust himself." Andrew bagged the books and handed them to Hachette.

"Drop by my office sometime this week. We'll continue the discussion."

~

Andrew was prepared for a smoke-filled, cluttered office, but that wasn't the case. Other than several books and magazines that lay on the end tables and his current project scattered about his desk, Hachette's literary treasures and notes were organized in the bookcase that ran the length of one wall or in the battered file cabinet that squatted in the corner behind his desk. Cool, fresh air from a cracked-open window circulated through the office.

"Thanks for stopping by," said Hachette as he set down his pen and walked from behind his desk to shake hands with Andrew. "Have a seat." He indicated a stuffed chair opposite his own and just as worn. Hachette offered Andrew a mug of coffee. Then he pulled a tin of cookies off his filing cabinet and placed it on an end table near Andrew's chair. "Help yourself." Sitting down with his own mug, Hachette said, "So, Morin has you stumped."

Andrew had just bit into a cookie and washed it down quickly with a sip of coffee. Hachette wasn't one for small talk.

"I couldn't wrap my mind around the ending. For someone unafraid to question, why was he so hung up on the norms of the Church at the end of his life?"

Hachette leaned back. "Change of perspective, perhaps. At your age, life extends indefinitely. Has anyone died in your immediate family?"

"My dad's parents. But they died when I was very young. I don't remember them."

"Well, as you get older, death becomes very tangible. What lies beyond death is more than a mere curiosity. And for all one's theological insight, it's hard to trust mercy, to relax in the unknown, in unconditional love. I believe that was Morin's quandary. Does he trust his experience of God or latch on to a set of tenets . . . just in case?"

Andrew looked at Hachette and shrugged. "Something to think about. Honestly, death hasn't been one of my top concerns." He had never had a professor taking him so seriously, like an equal. "Who are the note-takers?"

"The who?" Hachette looked up from the coffee he'd been sipping, surprised by the sudden shift in their conversation.

"Those students who write down every word that's said in class. What's up with them?"

"Oh, my friends from the Proclaimers of Christ—the PoCs. They're connected somehow with that youth group on campus. I believe they call it the FonS Student . . . something."

"The *FonS*?" Andrew said with surprise.

"You know of it?"

"Yeah, a little."

Hachette paused as if to allow Andrew to elaborate. But Andrew turned and picked up another cookie.

Hachette continued, "Let's just say that the PoCs have strong beliefs regarding what constitutes the Catholic faith and even stronger beliefs about those who they believe are teaching otherwise. Nothing would make them happier than to see me go into early retirement."

"So what are they doing with all their notes?"

"Who sifts through all their notes, I have no idea. On occasion the dean will call me into his office to update me on their reports. I have a couple of the PoCs in every class."

"It doesn't bother you?"

"They're entitled to their beliefs, I suppose. I think they have bigger problems of their own. I'm just a distraction."

"What do you mean?"

"It happened a few years ago. A young couple. They had been part of the PoCs early on, throughout their teens, I believe. Involved in all their youth outreach programs, went to college together, got married right after . . . maybe before graduating. In any case, a baby soon followed. They were looking for a new home, trying to find solid employment, and still involved in all the youth programs. Well, they go home for a baptism in the family and on the way home, the guy pulls over, shoots his wife, the baby and then himself."

This was not the ending Andrew anticipated. "Are you f—king kidding, me?"

"Yeah, that sums up how most of us felt. The poster couple for Catholic courtship and marriage. Hadn't shared a kiss before the *I do*, so they said. Spoke at the FonS youth conferences. The tragedy put the local PoCs in a tailspin. For one semester their members didn't show up in my classes. But they've come back with a vengeance since then."

"What! Why?"

"I thought the incident might create a moment of pause, you know, some institutional introspection, a little humility. But no, in the end the corruption of the world, the persecution of Catholics by the media, and the lack of solid Catholic teaching in the Church turned out to be the culprit." Andrew sat up in his chair, amazed. "Yes, it appears the only change the incident sparked was a more rigid adherence to the PoC regulations . . . code of conduct . . . whatever it is they follow."

"Why are they still allowed on campus?"

"It's not like one of the leaders is shooting the members. In the eyes of the hierarchy, the PoCs are fervent and faithful . . . outstanding evangelizers. According to the police, a deranged husband killed his family and himself. Seems he had made some threats—several incidents of abuse came to light after. But the wife was determined to make the marriage work. I don't know exactly what goes on within the group; but I sense there's a lot of pressure to be perfect Christian parents or the most fervent priests and nuns in the strictest orders. And, God forbid, they feel you threaten—or question—anything they espouse."

"Shit!" said Andrew thoughtfully. He looked at his watch and said as he stood, "Well, so much for chit-chat."

Hachette chuckled.

CHAPTER 20

"So glad the exams are over," yawned Mei-Lien.

Mei-Lien had just completed her run of final exams; Andrew had finished his the day before. With classes finished and exams coming to an end, the study rooms were readily available and reservations easily extended. So Mei-Lien and Andrew arranged one last rendezvous before Mei-Lien went back East with her parents. They chatted about their exams, happy with the results already posted and hopeful about those to come. It was a relief to get together without a stack of books and the pressure to study.

"Is it worth it?" asked Andrew after Mei-Lien commented on the intensity of her courses.

She thought a moment and then replied, "I've wondered if becoming a doctor is really what I want. Am I doing it just for my parents? But now I believe this path is the right one for me. There are so many specialties I can move ahead in."

"Like what?"

"Right now I'm thinking of women's issues—gyn—or a speciality in another field, but with a focus on women and children. In one of my courses this term, the prof gave a presentation showing how women were underrepresented in medical research. Research interests me . . . You know, my mom is one of the few women university math professors."

"Genius runs in your family." Genius or not, Andrew was relieved his undergraduate program did not require a class from Mei-Lien's mom.

Mei-Lien snuggled closer to Andrew. "I wish I could stay here for the summer or you could come with me."

"Like that would ever happen!"

Mei-Lien laughed. "We could meet at the FonS conference."

"I was talking to Hachette the other day. He said FonS is connected somehow to the Proclaimers of Christ—and they have some pretty messed up stuff going on."

"Never heard of them . . . From what I've gathered at the meetings, the FonS are just a college student organization. I know they're on other campuses in the country. That's why they've organized a big gathering for the summer, to bring young adults together from all over the US."

"So you are really going?"

"Not just me. The conference is going to be on the East Coast so my parents will be coming along. They're meeting with their Church in China group and plan to come to the conference's opening and concluding Mass."

Andrew wanted to tell Mei-Lien more of what Hachette had shared but Mei-Lien nestled even closer to Andrew. Her forehead was on his cheek. He could smell her shampoo and feel her soft, glossy hair on his neck. Andrew wrapped his arms more tightly around her as they leaned into a corner of the study room. He kissed her forehead.

With the library silent and empty, the pair became increasingly relaxed. As Mei-Lien returned the kisses, she gradually slid from her sitting position until both she and Andrew were locked in a continuous embrace on the carpet. Longing and the awareness that they would not be together for several months made them oblivious of everything except the affection and passion that stirred between them.

Neither heard nor saw the doorknob turn but they were catapulted out of their enchantment by a shriek right out of a Chinese opera.

CHAPTER 21

Mrs. Zhang stood over the pair as Andrew withdrew his hand from under Mei-Lien and Mei-Lien untangled her arms from Andrew's chest and neck.

"Mei-Lien!" Mrs. Zhang shrieked again. White rage stifled further invective. Her glare of raw abhorrence paralyzed Andrew as Mei-Lien got to her feet, grasped her backpack, and approached the door. Mrs. Zhang grabbed her by the shoulder, thrust her out of the study room and slammed the door with a force that rattled the picture on the wall. Andrew sat cross-legged, elbows on his knees, head in his hands, vacuous and inert. Never in his life had he experienced that level of outrage or naked hatred.

～

The living room became a courtroom without a defense team. Mrs. Zhang rained down accusations in Cantonese, Mandarin and English. Mr. Zhang, less voluble but equally disturbed, echoed and backed up Mrs. Zhang with the shake of his head and "Deceitful . . . How could you . . . after all you've been given."

"Sneaking, slithering snake! Going behind our backs," said Mrs. Zhang, her voice high and shrill once again. "If I had not found you when I did, God knows how far it would have gone!"

Mei-Lien was speechless and numb. She uttered not a syllable when peppered with, "How long?" "Where did you meet?" "Who is that boy?"

Accusations rained over her and washed through her, punctuated by "Stupid, stupid girl!" Although submerged in guilt, Mei-Lien internally balked at the principal assertion: "That boy is out for one thing and one thing only!" Mei-Lien knew this was not true.

When the "proceedings" finally ended. Mei-Lien walked silently upstairs to her bedroom. She lay listlessly on her bed and eventually fell asleep to the drone of her parents' voices below.

~

"Shit!" said Micah.

"That's putting it mildly," mumbled Andrew. It had taken him over two hours to walk across town to Micah's house and he was fortunate enough to find him at home packing up for his summer job in LA.

"What are you going to do about Mei-Lien?" Micah asked after some silence.

"What can I do? You think her parents are going to let me talk to her on the phone? Hand over letters from me? Allow me into the house?"

"You could try."

"Okay. You can hold the other end of the battering ram when I bash down the door. You weren't there," said Andrew more sharply than he intended. "Her mom hates me. I can't imagine what Mei-Lien is going through . . . She has no one to talk to."

"You don't know that."

Andrew shot Micah a glance. "What do you mean?"

"She went to high school. And you're not the only person on campus."

"What! The FonS ladies? You think they'll give her support? Don't count on it. Besides, guess whom I saw in the library as I left? Richard, looking rather smug."

"Andrew, you know he's a jerk. You're on his black list. Anyway, I wasn't talking about the FonS."

"Then who?"

"I don't know . . . relatives . . . friends she's made here."

"Her parents fled China, alone. There are no relatives. And *we* are the friends 'she made here'. I don't think you understand how strict her parents are."

∽

Andrew pulled down his baseball hat and walked nonchalantly past Mei-Lien's home. Yesterday he had tried to catch a glimpse of her, but now, in the evening dusk Andrew lost all hope. There was no sign of activity, no lights on in the house. She and her parents had left as planned.

CHAPTER 22

"So how's pre-med going?" Andrew asked the young woman who had come to the bookshop with a list of texts to purchase. As fall classes resumed, Andrew had been going out of his way to approach anyone searching for books with a list in hand. Finally, he had come across a second-year pre-med student.

"It's intense, but I expected that."

"Last year a girl . . . a Chinese girl, Mei-Lien, was in your program. Have you seen her this year?"

"Yeah, I think I know who you're talking about." The girl paused. "No, I haven't seen her yet."

Classes had resumed a week before and neither he nor Micah, nor anyone they asked, had seen Mei-Lien. There was one last place to check, but Andrew had been putting it off.

～

Same place, same hamburgers, awkward freshmen mingling with each other, sodas in hand. Andrew popped open a can and scanned the faces. The FonS barbeque for newcomers. Richard didn't seem to be around but Andrew spotted Casie chatting with a couple of young women.

"Casie, may I speak with you?" asked Andrew.

"I'm rather busy now," she said.

"It'll only take a minute."

Casie turned to the two freshmen, "I'll be back in a moment."

Andrew didn't bother with small talk. "Have you seen Mei-Lien?" he asked lightly.

"No."

"Do you know when she's coming back?"

Casie flicked off imaginary dust on her sleeve and crossed her arms, "No."

"Well, then. Okay. Enjoy the barbeque."

Casie walked back to the young women. Andrew turned and left, dropping the soda he had barely sipped in the garbage.

~

Andrew was bent over, stocking a lower bookshelf with newly arrived textbooks.

"Leave her alone!"

Andrew spun around, face-to-face with Mrs. Zhang.

"I hear you're making inquiries about Mei-Lien. She is not here. She is not coming back."

"Where is she?"

"Does it matter? She's happy and she doesn't want to continue any relationship with you." Mrs. Zhang passed Andrew a small envelope.

"My daughter has plans for her life. You tried to . . . to trip her up. You boys, you get what you want and walk away." Mrs. Zhang turned, then looked back at Andrew, "I know all about you *and* your family. Stay away." And she strode off.

~

Andrew passed the note to Hachette. Since their first appointment he had come regularly to chat with his professor and, as time went by, Andrew shared more about his personal life.

Andrew,

I've transferred to a college with a better pre-med program. Your friendship meant a lot to me. But now with distance and even heavier course load, it is better that we end it for now. I need to focus on my studies.

I wish you well.

Mei-Lien.

Hachette flipped over the card and back again. "This is it?"

"Yeah, that's it. Hand-delivered with one of Mrs. Zhang's specialty put-downs." Andrew looked down at the carpet. "The transfer has nothing to do with a better college."

"That goes without saying," replied Hachette.

"This is all my fault."

"How so?"

"Studying together."

"You forced Mei-Lien to study with you?"

"Of course not! She enjoyed studying together as much as I did. If only her mother hadn't caught us making out."

"If Mrs. Zhang had caught you eating popcorn together, the reaction would probably have been the same."

"What should I do?"

"What can you do? The ball is in Mei-Lien's court now. You have to wait and see if she wants to play."

Two months later, Andrew received a letter from Mei-Lien sent to the bookstore. As soon as his shift ended, he found a quiet spot near a copse of trees, leaned against a sturdy trunk, and tore open the envelope.

Andrew,

I've settled in at the student residence and have begun to feel at home. Everyone here is so friendly, kind and helpful. When my boxes arrived from home there were more people wanting to help than there were boxes to bring up to my room! One student in particular, Connie, is always around to give a hand or encouragement. So, you see, I'm already making friends.

It's been a few months and I've had a chance to reflect on our relationship and discuss it with one of our Guardians.

Andrew paused and reread the sentence. Guardians?

As much as we may have felt attracted to each other, it could not have been love. I went behind the backs of my parents and engaged in carnal acts that I'm ashamed of now. True love does not reside in deceit and lust. What we experienced was an illusion.

Who is this? thought Andrew.

I know you did not think highly of the Proclaimers of Christ *but I can assure you that they are a warm and Christ-filled organization. Their members have such an interest and concern for students that they open residences like mine to provide a safe and welcoming home away from home.*

Christ! Not the PoCs! Andrew sat down and pressed his back against the trunk. Could Mei-Lien have written this letter?

I hope you reconsider your opinion of the PoCs as they are unfounded.

I pray that your spiritual life will continue to grow and that weekly Mass becomes a necessity. Please do not try to contact me as I do not believe this will be in the best interests of you or me.

In Jesus our saviour,

Mei-Lien

Andrew dropped his hand with the letter and stared off in a daze.

PART TWO

CHAPTER 23

"The sun is out," said Rebecca as she opened the blinds of their apartment, "Let's go for a walk."

Andrew still looked haggard from the night before. The wine had loosened his tongue, unloading memories from years past, but did nothing for his mood and outlook. For Rebecca, walking amid nature cleared the mind and restored peace.

Initially the cold, crisp air made them shudder but they warmed as they picked up their stride and, in time, they loosened the scarves around their necks.

The lakefront path, about a twenty-minute walk from their apartment, extended for miles interspersed with parks, playgrounds, and tourist sites with eateries. When they reached the lake they paused to take in the view and then began to walk toward the city centre. Rebecca put her arm through Andrew's and he pulled her close. They walked in silence for some time and Rebecca could feel him relaxing.

"I'll go and speak to Mark Johnson on Monday. He may know what's up between Secure Star and the IFYA."

"Last night you didn't say a word about the International Festival for Young Adults . . . or the infamous Reverend Theo Augustine O'Rourke."

Andrew let out his breath, "Yeah, that all happened a few years later."

CHAPTER 24

"You got nothing to lose. Less than a year, all expenses paid."

Andrew toyed with the application form Theo O'Rourke had just handed him. "Thanks. I'll look it over."

"No paycheck, I know, but it will be a great experience." Theo made a sweeping gesture with his eyes around the college bookstore. "You don't want to stay here the rest of your life."

~

As planned, in three years Andrew had completed his business degree with a major in Human Resources. Working every spare moment at the college bookstore, renting a basement bedroom, and studying relentlessly to keep up his grades, Andrew retained his scholarships and managed to accrue very little student debt. In August, he'd slipped into a full-time position at the college bookstore that became available as he was completing the last of his exams.

Theo O'Rourke had finished his philosophy studies at the college. During those years he was considering a vocation to the priesthood and living at the diocesan House of Discernment. He was accepted by the local bishop as a candidate for the priesthood and for the past year or so was working toward his Masters of Divinity degree at the college, living in the same complex but in a wing called the House of

Formation for Priestly Vocations.

Theo had come to know Andrew through his visits to the bookstore and the two had spoken on occasion when Andrew went to Mass celebrated by Hachette. Theo was known around campus for promoting various and sundry causes that spanned participation in devotional practices, to religious concerts and conferences, to fundraising for obscure Catholic organizations.

However, Theo was right. Andrew did not want to settle into a career at the college bookstore. He considered his present job as a perch on which he could catch his breath, save some money and plan for the future. But he wasn't sold on Theo's proposition.

"I have to get back to work," Andrew said. "I'll let you know."

"Oh, and here's a poster you can hang on your window." Theo placed a rolled sheet of paper on the counter. Then he slung his black leather book satchel over his shoulder and walked out of the bookstore. At the door he turned and said, "Give it a shot. Like I said, you've got nothing to lose."

"What's he want us to do now?" said a clerk who had come up to the counter as Theo left, "Sell his sister's Girl Scout cookies?"

~

Hachette put on his glasses and took the application form that Andrew handed him. "So this is from O'Rourke. His latest cause, no doubt."

"International Festival for Young Adults. You know anything about that?" asked Andrew.

"Not much." Hachette flipped through the form, set it on the end table and removed his glasses. "From what I understand, it's a gathering of Catholic young people . . . like a rally, of sorts. Lots of concerts with Christian music. They're held in different countries. I believe two or three have been held so far. I don't know much more than that."

"The diocese is looking for volunteers on a managerial level," said Andrew. "Room and board is provided and free registration for the festival. No salary. But I would be getting experience that I wouldn't likely get at my age if I applied for a job. And the commitment is less than a year."

"Do you have any idea of what you'd be doing?"

"Theo said something about registrations."

Hachette glanced again at the application and shrugged.

"It's up to you. Sorry I can't help you more."

"Ah . . . There's just one other thing."

Hachette laughed. "There always is. Let's see, your mother is coming to town and needs a place to stay? You need a sandwich to hold you over until your next paycheck?"

Andrew smiled. Hachette had become a trusted advisor over the years and had even helped him with a few cafeteria vouchers when he noticed the amount of cookies Andrew was devouring during their meetings.

"I need a letter of recommendation from my pastor in order to apply."

"Oh, that's easy. Come by tomorrow."

CHAPTER 25

Mrs. Zhang entered the bookstore and walked down a random aisle. The shelves were low enough for her to look over and scrutinise most of the store. Andrew was pulling out a cart of books from a back room and she hastened to meet him before he reached the counter.

"So, you've done it again," she said, approaching Andrew from a side aisle.

"Excuse me?" said Andrew, both baffled and miffed. This was the first time Mrs. Zhang had said a word to him in over two years and he had no idea what she meant.

"Mei-Lien has been writing to you, hasn't she?" Mrs. Zhang stated.

Andrew was so astounded by the accusation he blurted, "Mei-Lien? Writing to me? Are you insane?"

Mrs. Zhang could see by Andrew's reaction that she had been entirely mistaken. There was no smirk, no assured retort, no indication he was in anyway prepared for her allegation. It was now Mrs. Zhang's turn to be discomfited and at a loss for words.

"I'm sorry . . . I truly am," she said as she turned and left the store.

～

"Leave the boy alone," Mr. Zhang said irritably. "He thought you were insane? He's right. That's what you are acting like."

"We're hearing less and less from Mei-Lien."

"Mei-Lien is twenty-one."

Mrs. Zhang stood in her husband's study looking out the window.

"We're still paying her bills."

"You worry too much," said Mr. Zhang.

"Mei-Lien didn't come home this summer and last year she only stayed a week."

"She told you, she went for a group study in Hong Kong and this year to Singapore."

"But study what? We never really know the details . . . just the cost."

"She said in her letter they would be visiting hospitals and hospices," said Mr. Zhang. "She is a medical student. It's good experience."

"I'm concerned."

"You're always concerned. You worried about her friends in high school, so we filled her days with piano, Chinese language, art, dance . . ."

"This is different."

Mr. Zhang refused to answer and returned his attention to the course work at his desk. After a few minutes, with his wife standing rigidly at the window, he said, "All your worries are going to blow over when you receive your next letter from Mei-Lien. They always do."

"Aren't you the least bit uneasy?"

Without looking up Mr. Zhang said, "Give her a call."

Mrs. Zhang knew it was useless to continue the conversation with her husband. She had tried to call, but Mei-Lien was either busy, not at the residence, or able to speak just a few moments before hurrying off to . . . something else.

CHAPTER 26

For almost two and a half years Mei-Lien had boarded at the Lantana. The residence came highly recommended by a mother Mrs. Zhang had met at the concluding Mass of the FonS summer conference.

Mrs. Zhang had been toying with the thought of transferring Mei-Lien to a university in the East that had a prestigious post-graduate medical program. Hearing about a residence for women that supported her values and study ethics made this option more tenable. The Lantana was situated within easy distance of the university and also a college, both of which Mrs. Zhang knew would be suitable for Mei-Lien's pre-med program. Mrs. Zhang had called the Lantana the day after the recommendation. Summer sessions were still in progress so the residence was open. A tour was offered for the next day.

Tension had been smouldering between Mei-Lien and her mom ever since Mrs. Zhang had intruded on her tryst with Andrew and forced her abrupt departure. She reluctantly accompanied her mother for the tour.

Their reception at the Lantana residence was warm and inviting. After introductions, they were invited to lunch. Mei-Lien sat among a group of residents while Mrs. Zhang sat at a table with two women who were responsible for the residence—Guardians, they were called. Occasional bursts of laughter came from the table of the students and Mrs. Zhang was happy to see Mei-Lien enjoying herself.

The Guardians asked Mrs. Zhang about her hopes for Mei-Lien which, in time, led to the devotion Mrs. Zhang had for the Church and her attachment to the Catholic community struggling in China. The last topic piqued the interest of the Guardians, prompting question after question. As Mrs. Zhang described her escape from China and eventual relocation in the US, they were in awe. They were particularly interested in the current state of the Church in China.

"Excuse me," said one of the students politely.

"Yes," said a Guardian.

"We'd like to take Mei-Lien on a tour."

"That would be fine." And the group of students left the dining area.

"And here I am, taking up your time," said Mrs. Zhang.

"Oh, continue," said the Guardian. "We have plenty of time."

A couple of young women in housekeeping dresses below their knees discreetly entered the room and began to clear the tables.

Mrs. Zhang and the Guardians talked for another half-hour until Mrs. Zhang once again protested that she could talk for hours on the subject but did not want to impose on them further. This time the Guardians did not urge her on. Instead they suggested a tour.

The library and study room, the bedrooms and community areas were as clean and beautifully arranged as the dining room and reception hall. If they passed a student in the hall, they were greeted with a wide smile.

"Are the girls always so well-groomed and welcoming?" asked Mrs. Zhang.

One the Guardians laughed lightly, "I'll pass on your compliment," she said. "But, yes, we do encourage both."

As they descended to the basement recreation and exercise room, Mrs. Zhang could hear the chatter and laughter of young women. Mei-Lien was playing table tennis with three other students and several others stood around cheering them on.

~

Later that evening when Mrs. and Mr. Zhang were alone in the guest room of a friend, Mrs. Zhang said, "You should have seen it! Everyone was so ... welcoming! The other girls took to Mei-Lien right away—very friendly and so polite. And the Guardians were extremely interested in the Church in China."

"The Guardians?" asked Mr. Zhang.

"That's what they call the women—the chaperones who run the residence," said Mrs. Zhang as she removed her earrings and necklace. "They belong to that Catholic group, Proclaimers of Christ. Seems they also run the FonS groups. Mei-Lien will have Catholic friends—girlfriends that aren't boy crazy: they keep an eye out for that."

Mr. Zhang loosened his tie, took off his shoes and lay propped up with pillows on the bed. From the attached bathroom, Mrs. Zhang continued, "They don't just accept anyone . . . The boarders are screened for good grades, good character, volunteering—Mei-Lien, remember, helped teach younger children Chinese at the cultural centre—that will help. The girls don't have to be Catholic, but most are, the Guardians said."

She emerged in her dressing gown and sat on the edge of the bed facing her husband.

"How much would all of this cost?" Mr. Zhang asked.

CHAPTER 27

Mei-Lien had been the subject of many private conversations between Mr. and Mrs. Zhang. Her involvement with "that boy from the bookstore"—Mrs. Zhang refused to say his name—startled both parents. They were both staunch on the point that there would be plenty of time for dating *after* her studies. Hadn't *they* studied assiduously to achieve the positions they held today? Besides, Mei-Lien was too young.

Having Mei-Lien continue at her current college held many advantages: it was a good program—not the best but good, Mei-Lien lived at home, and she received a discount on her tuition because her parents were full-time staff. Moving to a college on the other side of the country would mean full tuition and residence fees. While they could afford it, the cost would take a hefty slice from their savings for Mei-Lien's post-graduate medical program. And Mei-Lien would be so far away. Although the Zhangs were strict and demanding, they loved their daughter and would miss her.

Mrs. Zhang wanted to keep her daughter on track and, now that she had seen the residence, she was more comfortable sending her across the country to study. Besides, Mei-Lien would have to transfer to another university for her medical degree anyway. Maybe it was better she transfer now.

The Zhangs took Mei-Lien out to dinner and presented the possibility of her transfer. Mrs. Zhang anticipated resistance but she knew their proposal would be compelling. The previous year Mei-Lien had wanted to live in the dorms. Although Mrs. Zhang didn't know how serious Mei-Lien was with "that boy," she did know that living in the residence would be a huge incentive for Mei-Lien to transfer to the East.

There were two conditions to the transfer: a serious commitment to her studies and a pause in her "relationship" for a few years. If she and "the boy" both felt as strongly for each other after that period, they would not stand in her way. Mei-Lien agreed eagerly to the former and grudgingly to the latter.

By the end of July Mei-Lien was on the waiting list for the college and university. After applying to the Lantana residence and submitting Mei-Lien's grades and letters of recommendation, Mrs. Zhang was assured by the Guardians that Mei-Lien would have a bed if she was accepted. And as her plan fell into place that September, Mrs. Zhang felt relieved and blessed. But that was two years ago.

Mei-Lien's initial letters had shown a heightened religious sense, something Mrs. Zhang had savoured. But with time, the distance between her letters had become greater and phone conversations increasingly brief. In September Mei-Lien began her final year of pre-med and since that time, Mrs. Zhang had only received a couple of rushed calls to say she was fine and her studies were going well. Mrs. Zhang had begun to imagine that, with her graduation approaching in the spring, Mei-Lien was again in contact with Andrew. That delusion exploded with Andrew's reaction of utter disbelief.

CHAPTER 28

Toward the end of October Mrs. Zhang arrived home from work to find a letter from Mei-Lien in the mailbox. She dropped what she was carrying and slit open the envelope. It was an invitation to spend Christmas with Mei-Lien at the Lantana, a parent appreciation holiday from the twenty-third of December to January first.

Mrs. Zhang was taken aback. She had looked forward to having Mei-Lien home for three weeks over Christmas break and resented this intrusion. Yet, the invitation was very thoughtful. The list of festivities included midnight Mass at the cathedral and a full Christmas dinner. And she and her husband would be staying at the residence with Mei-Lien.

The more she thought of it, the more she warmed to the idea. They had visited Mei-Lien at the residence but had never really shared her life there. This would give them a chance to participate in her activities, meet her friends, come to know more about her summer trips and consider options for medical school. As she discussed the invitation with Mr. Zhang, to which he willing acquiesced, she had to admit once again that her worries had been unfounded.

CHAPTER 29

Office storage boxes were piled haphazardly around the desk, dates scribbled on the sides or lids. It was the end of November and registration forms were flowing in for the July International Festival for Young Adults.

"Here's your desk," said Theo O'Rourke. Due to his early effort to promote the International Festival for Young Adults at the local level, and his ability to navigate and accommodate Church leadership, Theo had landed a position within the IFYA organizing committee. This assignment was considered part of his priestly training—his year of pastoral ministry.

As one of the assistants to the IFYA executive director, Theo was responsible for Andrew's orientation to the national office as well as his new position managing the team of volunteers that processed registrations. The orientations for both were remarkably short. The first consisted of a tour of the executive offices, the chapel where the staff met daily for Mass, and the general office area: a cavernous room recently vacated by a failed phone order company. Its expansive carpet, pocked and worn, was interspersed with groups of mismatched desks laden with phones and desktop computers. Tangled bunches of cords draped the backs of the desks and ran across the floor vying for power strip bars and outlets.

"Those tables over there," said Theo pointing to a few rows of folding tables and chairs at the back of the large room, "you can use for your team meetings and meals. The kitchenette is in the corner there."

Seeing only a handful of people chatting or booting up their computers, Andrew asked, "Where is everybody?"

"I had you come in early. The main crew will be here in a half-hour or so."

Theo directed Andrew to the group of desks used for registrations and indicated Andrew's, the one surrounded by storage boxes.

"Zack," called out Theo, waving over a young man walking toward the desks with a cup of coffee. As Zack approached, Theo continued, "This is Andrew. He'll be heading up the team entering registrations. Would you show him the data entry program?" Then turning to Andrew, "You're going to do great. See you around." Zack saluted Theo's back as he turned away.

Ever since Andrew had begun his volunteer stint in October, the regional director of the IFYA in California had been impressed with Andrew: his ability to work with others as well as his efficiency in processing and forwarding their local registrations. So when a member of the national team left in November, Andrew was asked to leave the California division and oversee the processing of all the registrations pouring into the national office.

Andrew had arrived in the Midwestern hub the day before and was driven to his living quarters: an aging seminary with more rooms than candidates. An unused wing was designated for the IFYA male volunteers. Though old and musty, the arrangement was better than his shared quarters in California. His private bedroom here had a sink, and the large group bathroom meant no more waiting for a shower. Andrew considered it a luxury to have a hot breakfast and supper served daily in the seminary dining room, not to mention the prepared bagged lunch he picked up on his way out to work.

But any illusions of order and efficiency ended as Andrew surveyed the stacks of boxes. "Zack, what's all this?"

"Registrations to be processed. By the end of the day, there'll be at least another, if not two. The guy who left said he landed a job he couldn't pass up. But I think he was swamped."

Zack, as Andrew came to find out, was a jack-of-all-trades. He was the go-to person for IT issues and was willing to assist wherever he was needed. In the past few weeks he had spent a good deal of time with registrations. Zack sped through the explanation of the computer program for registrations, discovering at the onset that Andrew was already familiar with it. In California, Andrew had assisted parishes and groups as they filled out their forms, completing many on the computer if they came to the diocesan office. But the regional computers weren't linked so all the forms had to be printed out and the data entered at the national office.

Zack went on to explain that as the mailed or faxed registrations arrived at the national office, they passed through the hands of volunteers who dated each packet and withdrew the payments or payment information. The registration packets were then passed to the registration department. From the dates on the boxes, Andrew could see that they were backlogged at least one month.

Looking at the empty desks that were gathered near his, Andrew asked, "So how many are assigned to registration?"

"You and four others. I pitch in when I can. The others should be here soon." Leaning in closer, he added, "Angela's the best of the bunch."

~

Within a week Andrew and his team had tweaked their process. Andrew scanned the packets and distributed them to his team. Simple, problem-free registrations were given to Matt, Elizabeth and Juan for quick data entry. Andrew handled the complex English registrations and Angela, proficient in four languages, handled all other registrations with complications.

Initially the problems they encountered were time-consuming because they involved consultation with their supervisor and phone calls to the registrants. But as the days went by, both Andrew and Angela became more adept at resolving problems as similar situations repeated themselves. They developed a trouble-shooting manual, adding to it as their solutions were approved by their supervisor. By week three, an *esprit de corps* had developed among the registration team and they celebrated with day-old donuts when they began processing more registrations than those arriving. As they "clinked" their paper cups together, they calculated by Christmas they should only be a couple of weeks behind.

CHAPTER 30

The dining room was transformed by exquisite arrangements of evergreens, holly, poinsettias and candles. The lid of the grand piano was propped open and a resident in an evening gown gently fingered familiar Christmas hymns. Mei-Lien led her parents to their table and excused herself to help usher in other guests.

The holiday visit was proceeding beyond the expectations of Mrs. Zhang. After being warmly welcomed at the airport by Mei-Lien and a Guardian, the Zhangs had been lodged in a spacious guest room at the Lantana residence. Their quarters were arranged with finesse and meticulous regard for their comfort: on a round table near the window glistened a small fiber optic Christmas tree and, next to it, a fruit basket with bananas, mandarin oranges and pears intermingled with packets of Ningxia goji berries and Ziziphus jujube dates—all favourites of the Zhangs. On the opposite side of the room, set off with a brilliant red poinsettia, was a credenza with a plate of cookies, several bottles of spring water, an electric kettle, a couple of porcelain tea mugs with lids and a variety of high-end teas they used at home. Whenever the Zhangs left for an outing or event, they returned to a tidied room, a replenished fruit basket and cookie platter, clean mugs, and fresh towels in their private bathroom.

Their first two days were a whirl of activities: a visit to an art gallery, a walk through Mei-Lien's campus, shopping, viewing the city's Christmas lights and a performance by the city's philharmonic orchestra. One or two of Mei-Lien's friends accompanied them on these outings. Their conversations were invariably buoyant—chatting about past events, their courses and the week's upcoming enjoyments. The previous evening the residents, Guardians, the Zhangs and some other family and friends had been bussed to the cathedral for midnight Mass. At noon today, following a lavish brunch, they attended a Christmas Mass in the residence chapel. And now, the Christmas dinner!

Mei-Lien returned to the dining room, her arm interlocked with Connie, another resident. Mei-Lien introduced Connie's brother, Scott, and her parents, Mr. and Mrs. Tan, and explained that the Tan family would be seated together with the Zhangs for the evening. There were only five residents staying throughout the Christmas break and just three families sharing in the week's celebrations, yet the dining hall was filled: relatives and friends of the Guardians, some benefactors with their families, and several clergy who alternately celebrated the Mass at the residence occupied every available table.

A bell chimed and one of the priests blessed the food and led the prayer before meals. After they were served the first course, Mrs. Zhang said to Mrs. Tan, "I understand you are from China."

"Oh, generations ago. Our families have been in Singapore for ages. After our marriage, we transferred to the US—the Tan family wanted to expand its business. Both Scott and Connie were born here."

"Do you go back to visit?"

"Oh, yes, at least once a year. We have large extended family on both sides."

"That's fortunate. It's important for children to know their culture and language."

"Language . . . well . . . for the most part, we all speak English with a little dialect tossed in here and there. But we try to keep up with Mandarin for the sake of our business. Scott does fairly well. Connie is a little better. I understand Mei-Lien is quite proficient."

"Yes, both in Mandarin and Canton—"

Mrs. Tan turned abruptly toward her husband and Mr. Zhang on her right who were discussing the current state of the real estate market. "Don't forget the impact of . . ."

The rest of her statement melded with the chatter and music that filled the room. Mei-Lien, next to her, was turned toward Connie and Scott in a lively conversation. So Mrs. Zhang enjoyed her meal for a few minutes taking in the scene before her, particularly the servers in their pastel uniforms, silent and attentive, circulating among the tables to remove dishes, serve the next course, and refill the wine and water glasses.

"Oh, so sorry for the interruption," said Mrs. Tan, redirecting her attention back to Mrs. Zhang. "Sometimes my husband leaves out important information. He forgets not everyone is familiar with international real estate market. Are you enjoying your visit with Mei-Lien? As I understand," Mrs. Tan said under her breath, "she's one of the star residents."

"We are very proud of her," said Mrs. Zhang modestly. "And yes, our stay has been wonderful. The Guardians have taken such care to make sure we are comfortable and entertained. And the guest room is just beautiful."

"It should be," laughed Mrs. Tan. "My husband and I donated the funds to remodel the whole place." She gestured with her hand to encompass the entire residence.

"That was very generous of you. Why, you should be staying in our guest room!"

"Oh, nonsense! We always reserve a suite in a hotel uptown when we visit. We want the guestrooms to be used by those who are not able to afford such accommodations. Actually," she said, softening her voice, "we prefer it." Just then Mr. Tan let out a laugh, distracting his wife once again as she turned to find out what prompted his reaction.

"Our men are certainly hitting it off," said Mrs. Tan as she turned back to Mrs. Zhang. "My husband is such a charmer—makes friends at the drop of a hat." She took a couple bites of dinner and, as if responding to a question, continued, "The family business is in commodities—brokers and consultants—but Mr. Tan likes to dabble in real estate . . . Actually, I'm being modest: he is quite good. He helped negotiate a property deal for the extension of the archdiocesan offices and a contract for the renovation of the old seminary buildings. As the saying goes, (Here Mrs. Tan gave Mrs. Zhang a sidelong glance.) 'It's not what you know but whom you know.'" She smiled, hastily took another bite and went on, "He and the archbishop are great friends. The archbishop arranged a private audience with the Pope for our entire family last fall. What a blessing for us all! Mr. Tan and I pledged our fidelity to the Holy Father when he spoke with us. We could feel his holiness as he smiled at us and shook our hands—Oh, I have it here!"

Mrs. Tan reached for her bejewelled clutch and pulled out a slim wallet. "You'll see the moment . . ." She opened the wallet, quickly flipped past a couple of pictures, and stopped at a miniature of herself and her husband, slightly bent and smiling widely as the pontiff squeezed both of their hands. "Oh, I can still feel the moment as I look on this photo—we have a much bigger one framed at home. The Pope said he had heard of our commitment to the Church. What an honour!"

Mrs. Zhang had a brief reprieve from Mrs. Tan's medley of information, recollections and opinions when the soft-spoken servers brought over the entrées. She was alternately in awe of the Tans' contributions to the Church, irked by the patronizing tones, astounded by their business acumen and wealth, and repelled by the ostentation.

"Now tell me what it is that you do," said Mrs. Tan as she cut into her turkey. But before Mrs. Zhang could respond, she said, "Oh, yes, Mei-Lien told us on our last visit—university professors. Math, no less! I should hire you to calculate the odds on some of our bids!" Then turning her attention to Scott, she whispered, "Now, Scott, he is a smart boy. Been working alongside his dad for years, even during his studies. He's a great asset to the business."

Mrs. Zhang glanced at Scott: stout with closely cropped hair, leaning in toward Connie and Mei-Lien, gregarious, confident, engaging them both as he spoke. The girls laughed, contradicted some outrageous statement he had made and laughed again.

"Will Scott be joining us for the historical tour tomorrow?"

"Oh, no! Tomorrow we're flying out for our annual Christmas vacation in Anguilla. Connie will be back in time for school, of course."

"Anguilla?"

"Oh, it's the loveliest of the Caribbean islands! You've never been? You must go sometime and when you do . . ."

Mrs. Zhang caught the eye of one of the servers and raised her wine glass for a refill.

~

"How about coming home for a week before classes start?"

It was the day before their departure and Mrs. Zhang was making her last attempt to convince Mei-Lien to spend a few days in California. "You'll have a break from the snow and cold."

But it was useless. Mei-Lien was doing research for a thesis due at the end of the spring term that, she insisted, would give her a boost in her post-graduate studies. Her university applications were in for medical school but she wanted to complete a couple more submissions for scholarships. So reluctantly Mrs. Zhang let her hope, sparked by the Tans' family trip to Anguilla, expire.

CHAPTER 31

Mrs. Zhang had spoken with Mei-Lien a couple of times in the past month, briefly, of course, but both initiated by Mei-Lien. So when she found a hand-addressed letter among the bills in mid-February, she was both surprised and delighted. She dropped her handbag on the kitchen table and opened the envelope.

Dear Mom and Dad,

I know how busy you both are now with mid-term papers and exams and I'm keeping you close in prayer. Although very busy as well with schoolwork, I can't help but admire the beautiful snow-clad evergreens as I walk to my classes. God's creation is magnificent and leads me to praise Him continually. And considering the grandeur of God, I want to share with you a decision I've made which is of the utmost importance for my life now and eternally.

Mrs. Zhang felt her breath catch and her hand clench the letter. She quickly read on to the following sentence.

It has been some time that I have felt drawn to make a fuller commitment to the Proclaimers of Christ.

"What?" she gasped. Mrs. Zhang reread the sentence. "Commitment? You're a boarder! We pay your fees!"

For the past couple of years I have been among the Initiates. I have now committed to a more advanced level with the Invested.

"Initiates? Invested?" Mrs. Zhang let the letter fall to the table. She stood, walked to the window looking out on the patio and wiped her clammy hands on her skirt. After some moments she forced herself to refocus, returned to her chair and continued to read Mei-Lien's letter.

Through this commitment I have more deeply embedded myself in Christ and His Church.

I know you were looking forward to my coming home after final exams for an extended holiday; however, with my commitment comes new responsibilities and I will no longer be able to come home.

A volley of Chinese expletives fired through the kitchen. Tears welled in her eyes and her heart pounded in anger as she read on.

This is a sacrifice for me as well as for you but we do it willingly for Christ and in the end we will have a heavenly recompense. I wanted to tell you in advance so that you will not purchase the tickets.

My studies are going well and I know that you will be proud of my marks. I am tutoring Chinese children in both Mandarin and Cantonese and frequently give presentations to their parents.

Must go now for our evening prayer. God bless you.

Your loving daughter,

Mei-Lien

Mrs. Zhang walked in a daze to the living room, putting some space between her and the sheet of paper that bore the stilted vestige of her daughter. She was furious with the Guardians who had overwhelmed her with their attentiveness and hospitality at Christmas, dulling her misgivings. She now saw it all as a ploy in a quest for the commitment of her daughter to their organization.

"How could I have been so stupid! How could Mei-Lien be so stupid!" No sooner had she uttered the words, than a realization so incriminating had her sinking into the sofa. Stupid girl—that's what she, in anger, had called Mei-Lien many times when her daughter seemed unfocused or naïve. And then with Andrew. Stupid girl. She had pushed and prodded and, ultimately, her daughter had obeyed. She was the one who had forced Mei-Lien into the Lantana residence, into the arms of the Guardians and the clutches of the Proclaimers of Christ. Who was she to call Mei-Lien stupid?

CHAPTER 32

As instructed, Mrs. Zhang bowed her head along with the twenty or so persons gathered in the old church hall. When the lengthy oration finished she sat in the battered folding chair that creaked in protest when she shifted her position. Mrs. Zhang had hoped she could blend into the group of inquirers but, looking around, she realized this would not be the case. The participants were fewer than she expected and Mrs. Zhang had no idea how many were already members. It didn't matter. She had survived the Chinese Cultural Revolution—she knew how to disappear in the background.

~

Mrs. Zhang was born into a Chinese Catholic family. With Mao's rise to power, their faith had been forced underground. From her earliest years, Mrs. Zhang had learned to trust no one outside her immediate family. In school, she was silent and submissive as her parents had instructed: be a tree among trees in the forest, never the highest; be a goose among geese flying in formation, never in the lead. She dared to excel only in academics, but even there, just behind the top student to avoid jealousy.

The Chinese university she had attended hired her as an assistant professor. About this time, at a rare, clandestine Mass, she recognized

Mr. Zhang. He was an assistant professor in the Science department but Mrs. Zhang had never known he was a fellow Catholic caught up in the same charade. At the height of the Cultural Revolution, the two professors managed a risky escape to Hong Kong. With their connections to the Chinese Catholic community, they found asylum in the US and married shortly after. And now, here she sat at an inquiry session, seeking membership among the Proclaimers of Christ, preeminent, she was being told, among the new church Movements.

~

When her fury and feelings of betrayal had abated, Mrs. Zhang knew that she alone was to blame for Mei-Lien's involvement in the Proclaimers of Christ. She had separated Mei-Lien from family and friends to preserve . . . to preserve what? Mei-Lien had always been a good daughter and she, her own mother, had driven her away. Why? Because Mei-Lien had not measured up to an impossible standard that Mrs. Zhang had for herself. No, she alone was to blame and the humiliation of this realization nearly crushed her.

It was a burden she bore alone. Mr. Zhang had been charmed during their Christmas visit and enjoyed the camaraderie of the Tans. Mrs. Zhang foresaw that any reproach of the PoCs to Mei-Lien would only entrench her more deeply in the organization and into the dissembling arms of the Guardians—Mei-Lien was one of their favourites after all. The preferential treatment that had been lavished on them over the holidays had flattered and obliged a debt of gratitude but now Mrs. Zhang saw it as nothing more than a ruse to keep Mei-Lien away from home, just as the international studies had been during the summer breaks.

So, rather than push against Mei-Lien's decision, Mrs. Zhang decided to discreetly become a member of the PoCs. No one knew of her decision, neither Mr. Zhang nor Mei-Lien. She drove to a neighbouring town to avoid the PoCs on campus. Eventually, she was sure, all concerned in the organization would know—she was familiar with totalitarian regimes— but initially she could make her inquiries and come to understand the machinations of the organization incognito. Most importantly, she hoped being a member would allow greater access to Mei Lien—and she was willing to jump through the hoops of the now despised church Movement in order to maintain a relationship with her daughter.

CHAPTER 33

Andrew was visiting one of his aunts on a rare weekend off and called home at her insistence. "Surprise your mom," she had said. But the person who answered the phone was neither his mom nor his dad.

"Micah?" asked Andrew incredulously.

"At your service! How can I help you?"

"Micah! Why aren't you at college?"

"Spring break, my friend. Your mom signed me up for a landscaping gig—a week of spring clean up. And I'm finishing off some papers that will be due when I get back." Then laughing he said, "I have the back bedroom all to myself! By the way, your mom and dad just stepped out for groceries. Should be back in about an hour."

Since his Christmas visit several years ago, Micah had become part of the Covick family. Andrew's mother called him "my other son" and Micah called her "Mom-Sonia." He was concluding his final year of college and was aiming for a Masters in Creative Writing.

"What's up with you?" asked Micah.

"I'm visiting one of Mom's sisters."

"Your mom was saying that she hoped you'd be able to visit some of her family while you were out there."

"I just got a letter from Hachette."

"Yeah, I see him from time-to-time. Always asks about you."

"You'll never guess what I found inside the letter."

"Astound me."

"A letter from Mrs. Zhang."

"NO SHIT!" Andrew pulled the phone away from his ear.

"You better not be f—king with me!" exclaimed Micah.

"No joke," said Andrew.

"She's still stalking you?"

"This letter was really . . . unusual. Don't ask me what happened, but she was very apologetic. Said how sorry she was about her treatment of Mei-Lien and me, and how mistaken she had been about my character."

"That's it?"

"Pretty much."

"Are you going to get in contact with Mei-Lien?"

"I don't know . . . She was pretty clear about breaking up . . . maybe . . . I have to think about it."

Neither spoke for a few moments.

"When are you coming home?" asked Micah.

"I'll be finished with this job the middle of July." Then, with a change of tone, "Why don't you sign up for the IFYA? If you come as a volunteer, it's cheaper—Hachette will vouch for you. I'll have you assigned with me."

"What are you going to be doing?"

"Who knows. This place is not the epitome of organization. It's already March and, according to Theo O'Rourke—"

"O'Rourke?" Micah interrupted.

"Yeah, the guy's got his finger in every pot."

"I thought he was going to be a priest."

"That's still on. This is some kind of pastoral assignment. He continues his studies next fall. Anyway, as I was about to say, it's already March and Theo let slip that the priest in charge still doesn't know how they are going to house everyone. According to Theo, all will be in order by June. All we've been told officially is that the leaders of each youth group will be given the address of their accommodations when they check in."

"And this is supposed to encourage me to come?"

"Come on, Micah. If nothing else, it'll provide great writing material."

"I'll think about it."

"Just two weeks of your summer."

A month later, Micah capitulated and sent his volunteer application directly to Andrew. Through connections he had made over the past months, Andrew had Micah processed and claimed as a personal assistant.

CHAPTER 34

It was Friday, the beginning of June. For the past couple of months, Andrew and his team had been putting in twelve to fourteen hour days in order to keep up with the onslaught of registrations. Now, though the registrations were still arriving, the numbers were decreasing: the July festival was fast approaching.

"It's four o'clock," Andrew said to his team. "Tonight everyone is out of here by four thirty. Go do something fun . . . relaxing. And no one comes in tomorrow before noon." Within a half hour, the desks were empty except for Andrew's.

Over the past months, Andrew had had no time for anything other than eat, sleep and try, unremittingly, to keep abreast of wave upon wave of registrations. At night he collapsed on his bed and, at times, fell asleep without having kicked off his shoes. But now that the pace had settled down, he wanted to clear up a question that had been dogging him for the past month. In sorting out problematic registrations, a particular coordinator's name reoccurred once, twice, then again and again. This afternoon Andrew was determined to puzzle out this peculiarity.

With Zack's help, he had become adept at the search capabilities of the computer program and entered the name of the coordinator. Sure enough, over sixty group registrations appeared. Each group had additional co-coordinators, so the supervision was properly covered, but that's not what bothered Andrew. Though in the same country, the registrations were from four different organizations. Why did they all have the same lead coordinator? Andrew might not have been so quick to pick up on the discrepancy had not two of the organizations been the Proclaimers of Christ and the FonS Student Association.

"Hey! What's up?" called out Theo as he walked toward the executive offices with a fresh cup of coffee.

"Just trying to figure out what's going on with some registrations. I have the same lead coordinator for four different organizations. It doesn't make sense. It seems very unlikely that there are four coordinators with the same name."

"It makes perfect sense!" exclaimed Theo as he looked over Andrew's shoulder.

"But how can one person submit registrations for all these different organizations?"

"Because they're all branches of the Proclaimers. You didn't know that? The FonS are a college group—you must have met them at—"

"Yes," said Andrew cutting Theo off. "I knew the FonS had connections with the PoCs but didn't know it was the same organization."

"Well, the other two," said Theo looking at Andrew's printout, "Fidelis and Gratia, are for teens. One group—I can't remember which one—is for teens who are children of PoCs and the other is some kind of initiation for teens, you know, for beginners . . . something like that. They even have one for kids."

Andrew had already looked up the number of those registered from the four groups throughout the world. "Theo, there are tens of thousands coming from these four organizations alone."

Theo laughed. "There'd better be!"

"Why?" Andrew was completely bewildered.

"Because the Proclaimers of Christ are one of the key sponsors of the IFYA. They guarantee that a certain number of youth from their organizations will be coming."

"What?" Andrew blurted.

"Oh, they're not the only ones." Theo listed a handful of other church Movements. "And each of *them* has several branch groups as well."

Andrew grabbed a sheet a paper. "Let me get this straight." With Theo standing over him providing the details, Andrew outlined what looked like family trees.

"So you're telling me these six church Movements have over . . . let's see . . ." Andrew counted the organizations listed on the sheet before him, "Twenty-six organizations directly connected to them?"

"More or less. These are the groups I know off-hand."

"How do you even know all these groups?" exclaimed Andrew.

Theo seemed pleased his expertise was being recognized. "Because, you idiot, without them, we'd never be able to pull off a youth festival this size! The executive director was just on the phone yesterday thanking some of the leaders for their support and number of participants they registered."

"So, are you telling me the IFYA is basically a huge shindig for a handful of church Movements?"

"I wouldn't put it that way," said Theo, back-pedalling his initial enthusiasm to share information. "I mean you don't have to be a member of a church Movement to attend. But the leaders of these Movements always guarantee a certain number of participants."

From his experience with the FonS, Andrew could well imagine how these Movements corralled their members into attending.

"I'd better be going," said Theo. "You going to be here much longer?"

"I'll be off soon."

As Theo walked back to the executive offices, Andrew, sitting upright on the edge of his chair, began tracking the total number of participants from each organization that Theo had named. Seventy-five percent of those registered came from six church Movements! Andrew dropped back into his chair and pushed away from his desk. *What the hell have I gotten myself into?*

~

In the days that followed, during the meals and breaks, Andrew discreetly asked his companions around the table how they came to be long-term volunteers for the IFYA. Andrew knew that Angela, a recognized linguist, had been active in the campus ministry of her college and was recruited by her chaplain. Three of the others on his team were members of various church Movements as were many of the other volunteers he surveyed.

As he wrapped up his service for the IFYA, Andrew couldn't shake the nebulous feeling that he had been duped.

CHAPTER 35

Every week the appeals at the PoC gatherings became more urgent and Mrs. Zhang more irritated.

"The Pope has called us to evangelize and what better way than by sending our young people to the IFYA? Our children will be inspired and, through their example and conversations, they will evangelize the troubled youth of our time."

The leader raised a basket and shook it. "The Founder is counting on all of us. Thousands of our young people from all over the world have been registered for the IFYA but we still need the funds for the plane trips and fees. We are printing thousands of brochures on the teachings of Christ in ten different languages! Our work of evangelization cannot go ahead without your financial assistance. Do any of you want to be responsible for a young person who does not come to know Christ, who lives a life of sin? Be generous!"

He set the basket in the hands of a PoC seated nearby and, as it slowly circulated, he continued to expound. "What is money? The mammon that puts a wedge between us and God. How often we cling to it only to throw it away on frivolities—a fancy coffee, a worthless trinket, a pizza because we are too lazy to cook a decent meal. Dig deep, dig deep and give back your money to God from whom you received it."

Mrs. Zhang rankled as she wadded up a dollar bill in her purse and tossed it into the basket when it came around. She watched in disbelief as the woman next to her, apparently with no cash to spare, removed her watch and dropped it into the basket. She saw the leader, who was closely watching the progression of the basket, smile his approval at the woman. Despite their professed distaste for mammon, Mrs. Zhang noted that the PoC leaders certainly revelled in receiving it.

As she walked to the parking lot after the meeting, Mrs. Zhang continued to stew. Mei-Lien should have been home now, enjoying time with her family before beginning her graduate studies. Instead, as an "Invested" among the PoCs, she was spending this time arranging accommodations for thousands of PoC young people coming for the IFYA. More importantly, Mei-Lien had told her mother shyly, she had the honour of translating the Founder's writings and transcribing his sermons into Chinese so they could be widely distributed and brought back home to Chinese-speaking communities. Mrs. Zhang had listened dispirited. All the weekends spent in Chinese language schools, year after year, now at the service of the PoCs.

CHAPTER 36

The tables at the far end of the IFYA work hall were dressed with festively coloured tablecloths. Caterers brought in covered trays of food for the luncheon following the ceremony. At the opposite end of the hall a large folding table had been transformed into an altar. The tops of the desks were straightened and the work at hand tucked away in desk drawers. At noon, an archbishop from the Vatican processed in with a host of priests and the local bishop for a special Mass of Thanksgiving. The work hall was packed with the staff from the executive offices, the long-term volunteers, and others invited to the celebration for their connection to the IFYA. There were a limited number of chairs, so many of the volunteers remained standing or sat on the desks near the back. Among them stood Andrew, leaning against the wall. With just two weeks until the IFYA, this would be the last Mass celebrated with the executive staff and the long-term volunteers.

"We are gathered today in thanksgiving for your overwhelming generosity," said the archbishop as he began his homily. He spread out his arms and gestured emphatically toward all present, "Without you, this marvellous initiative, the International Festival of Young Adults, could never come to life. I have been informed of the hundreds of thousands who will attend this event—truly a miracle of God. This is living proof that the Church is very much in touch with the young people of our time!" Enthusiastic applause and cheers exploded from the participants.

DAWN THROUGH THE SHADOWS

Andrew closed his eyes. In touch with *what* young people? A representative slice? Or kids coming with a very specific viewpoint? Maybe the Church leaders should be looking at who's *not* coming.

His mind went back to his college days when the bishop came to celebrate the Mass at the opening and closing of the school year. After Mass, as the bishop processed out of the church he was swarmed by the smiling members of the FonS Student Association.

At the national office, Mass was celebrated every day in the chapel. However, once a week at noon an altar was set up in the large work hall. All work ceased and a vibrant liturgy was celebrated. Andrew was inspired and uplifted during these celebrations of faith, united with the other volunteers in the desire to share God's love with the world. Occasionally, a bishop would be the main celebrant and Andrew noted that this bishop, too, would be swarmed after the celebration. Previously Andrew thought the "group hug" was merely the enthusiasm of the volunteers. But now he wondered if it was not the same fawning he'd sensed at the college Masses.

Was the IFYA just another group hug from several church Movements, only a few hundred thousand times larger and with the Pope as the main celebrant? Was this really about reaching out in love to all young people or a quest to impress the watching world with numbers?

CHAPTER 37

The janitor wiped off the sweat dripping from his brow as he flipped through his wad of keys. "It's one of these," he said more to himself than to Andrew and Micah who stood behind him. After a couple of failed attempts he pushed opened the door of the antiquated elementary school gym. A gush of sweltering air, infused with decades of school lunches, spilt milk and aging floor wax, overwhelmed their senses. The draft from the open door sent tufts of dust and pollen twirling across the floor like tumble weed, picking up crumbs and wrappers as they scuttled across the expanse of the room. Dozens of rolled sleeping bags and backpacks were stacked against the walls.

"How many people are sleeping here?" asked Andrew.

"I don't know. I was called in yesterday evening to open the doors for a group of people coming for the big festival."

"Did anyone prepare for them?" asked Andrew.

"Did anyone even know they were coming?" added Micah.

"Well, by the looks of it, I'd say no," he said with a chuckle. Then looking at the confused faces of Andrew and Micah, he added defensively, "I take care of the church buildings. The school janitor closes down the school building in June. He comes back a few weeks before school starts to spruce the place up."

"So what do we have to do to get this place cleaned?" asked Micah.

"The pastor will be back in an hour or so . . . I'm in the middle of getting the church hall set up for another event."

Andrew threw a sidelong look at Micah who nodded. "Where are the brooms?"

~

"What the hell is going on?" barked the man silhouetted in the doorframe.

Andrew and Micah, stripped down to their denim shorts, were sweeping up the piles of dirt they had amassed with their broom and dust mop.

Andrew dropped his broom and Micah, his dustpan, as they walked toward the looming figure, wiping their sweating palms on their shorts as they went.

"Andrew Covick and Micah Baker, from the IFYA office," said Andrew extending his hand. "We're here to sort out a misunderstanding about the accommodations for some participants."

"A *misunderstanding*?" boomed the man, now clearly seen by his clerical collar as the pastor. "*Some* participants?" he laughed sardonically. "More accurately, over a hundred young people and their chaperones arriving yesterday evening and no one here having a clue they were expected!"

Speechless, Andrew and Micah stared at the gray-haired, Church veteran as he continued his tirade.

"Can you imagine trying to *sleep in this place*? It's hotter than hell. And those damn windows we've been trying to replace," he pointed, exasperated, at the large, paned windows lining the walls near the ceiling, "we only managed to open two. Those confounded pulley strings, all tangled and knotted." Then flaring up in anger with another thought, "And have you seen the bathrooms? Yes, the toilets and urinals six inches from the floor! Men have to kneel to take a pee! And only three stalls each for men and women? I gave them access to the whole damn school so they could at least wash their faces before midnight! To hell with security!"

Andrew and Micah had both winced when they checked the bathrooms, as much for the size of the toilets as for their uncleanliness and lack of toilet paper and paper towels.

"And what do you suppose I was doing this morning besides preparing for a funeral? Scouring the supermarkets," he roared, "for cookies, granola bars and juice to give these kids something to eat before they left for the festival—by the way, a trip on public transit that would take them at least two hours! Oh! And what have I been doing since the funeral? I've been begging the fitness club down the street to let the kids use their showers at night and a couple of restaurants to give them breakfast!"

His wrath somewhat depleted, the pastor scanned the hall, now freshly swept, all the windows opened, and the two young men before him, drenched in sweat, covered in dust and grime.

"Have you boys had lunch?" asked the pastor brusquely.

"No."

"I'll give you a hand with those dust heaps and then you can come with me to the rectory. I'm Fr. Joe."

~

Later, freshly showered, Andrew and Micah sat at the kitchen table of the rectory. Fr. Joe set down the platter of sandwiches he'd been preparing while they washed up and asked, "What do you want to drink? I have cold beer."

"Beer!" said Andrew and Micah in unison.

The pastor handed them each a bottle and popped the lid off one for himself. "You're going to need a few more of these before this hootenanny's over." He asked Andrew and Micah where they were from and how they had become involved in the IFYA. After sharing the information, Andrew went on to explain their current assignment.

"Micah and I were pulled from registrations this morning to handled a couple of . . . complications that the accommodation team couldn't deal with by phone."

The pastor shook his head. "I'm sorry I landed into you earlier. To be honest, I consider the IFYA to be an overblown, poorly organized, emotional hullabaloo with an exorbitant price tag. Then to have those poor kids unloaded at the school last night . . . And I, the last person who wanted to be involved. Your director got an earful this morning." He took a long swig of beer. "And then he sent you boys out here to straighten things out . . . my God. As if you had anything to do with the planning."

"So what do you have against the IFYA?" asked Micah as he bit into his second sandwich.

"I've always had my misgivings. But I have a sister who was a great supporter of the IFYA—anything papal for that matter. She and her husband travelled with their three teens to the last festival and the horror stories they came home with! Among them, accommodations like our gym. Their youngest got sick the second day, so she returned to their lodgings at a church hall while her husband and sons continued with their group. But when she arrived, my sister wasn't allowed to enter: the church hall was closed until nine every night for security reasons. She's in a different country, doesn't know the language, hauling around a sick kid. She manages to buy some ice and drinks and walk to a nearby park, trying to stay cool under the trees but close enough to a garbage can where my niece vomited as needed. That's just one tidbit I'll share. Needless to say, she's no longer on the bandwagon. The whole business needs to be reconsidered."

"Are all the accommodations like this one?" asked Micah.

"Some people hit the jackpot, like the four kids staying with the Donati family down the street. Each of those lucky buggers has their own bed in an air-conditioned house. I hear Mrs. Donati has a buffet planned for each morning.

"But the majority are not so fortunate. They wind up on the floors of a church hall or school gym where there is supposedly a team to watch over the facilities and make sure the kids have at least some muffins and a beverage to start the day.

"And then there are the poor schmoes who get dumped on unsuspecting parishes—it's the luck of the draw, my friends. People who can afford it pile into hotels. Which leads me to another problem I have with the IFYA—the cost.

"Did you know that the main stage for the closing Mass costs millions to construct? That's not including all the security lights, partitions, port-a-potties, etc., etc. that are needed for the hundreds and thousands of participants. And that site is used for less than twenty-four hours! And here we are with a dilapidated school and a church in need of repair. I can barely afford to squeeze out a stipend for our organist and youth minister let alone find funds for special education at the school. Yes, I have plenty of misgivings about the IFYA."

As Andrew and Micah finished off their sandwiches, Fr. Joe packed up some fruit and snacks and asked about their next appointment. Andrew showed him the address. "Let me give Max a call. He's a retiree and may be able to give you two a lift."

Fifteen minutes later they were shaking hands with Fr. Joe and sliding into Max's sedan.

"We really appreciate this," said Andrew to Max. "It took us an hour and a half to get here this morning on public transportation."

"Yes, the whole city is snarled in traffic with this festival going, but at least you'll be a little cooler in the car."

～

The next muddle on Andrew's list was simpler: a family had signed up for five participants to sleep in their basement and ten showed up at their door. Four were over eighteen years old and part of a larger group that reassembled each morning at the festival site. The others were younger and accompanied by a chaperone. Using the woman's phone, Andrew and Micah arranged for these six to join other participants lodging at a parish hall several blocks away.

"This couldn't have been handled from the office?" asked Micah as he and Andrew began their long trek to the festival central site.

"The lady had an accent. Maybe the person who answered the phone couldn't understand her. Who knows? I'm beyond trying to figure things out."

Three hours later the two friends trudged into the IFYA site office to give their report.

"How's it going?" asked a jubilant voice behind them. Before they could turn around, Theo had squeezed in between them, his arms around their shoulders.

"Well, it could be going a whole lot better for some of the participants," replied Andrew. He went on to describe the situation at Fr. Joe's parish. "How could more than a hundred people be assigned to St. Mary's parish without the pastor aware of it?" Andrew asked.

"It's a St. Mary's," said Theo. "There are half a dozen in the diocese. Somehow it got on the list. But in the end, everything fell into place—it was meant to be!"

"Well, everything didn't just *fall* into place," said Andrew. "Fr. Joe did a lot to straighten out the situation."

"As he should have. We all have to do our share to evangelize young people."

"Don't you think we owe him an apology and the participants as well?" interjected Micah. "That gym was so hot and absolutely filthy, I'd be amazed if anyone slept at all last night. We managed to get all the windows open today and when we left, Fr. Joe was trying to gather up some fans."

"The people who signed up for accommodations knew they weren't getting a five star hotel. This is a pilgrimage. Sacrifice is part of the package."

"Huh?" Micah and Andrew looked at each other.

"Theo! Are you coming? We're leaving now!" hollered a young priest from the other end of the hallway.

"On my way!" Theo shouted back. Then to Andrew and Micah, "There's a car leaving for the concert. Talk to you later."

Micah gazed at Theo as he trotted down the hallway to catch up with his friend. Andrew nudged him toward the door. "I'm too tired for this. Let's go pick up our dinner package."

CHAPTER 38

Andrew and Micah sat on a bench to eat their boxed dinner. Andrew had already told Micah about the PoCs and other church Movements behind the IFYA, which, unlike Andrew, Micah found very amusing. "You can't get away from these guys! Right back in the spider's web!" he had laughed. It only made him more curious about the unfolding of the IFYA.

"What's going on tonight?" asked Micah as Andrew pulled a program from his backpack.

"We missed the opening ceremony this afternoon but tonight there's a huge concert—that's where Theo's headed. We'll arrive late, but we can watch from the aisles as volunteers."

"Where is it?"

"At the stadium. We can catch a bus."

"Let's eat on the way."

The bus stop was mobbed. Andrew and Micah waited with the others, finishing off their dinner. Three buses en route to the stadium passed with a blaring horn, packed to the hilt.

"We'll be here all night at this rate," said Andrew. "We might as well walk."

An hour later, Andrew and Micah knew they were getting closer the stadium. First came the cheers, growing louder and louder with every block they walked. Then throbbing music from a Christian rock band spilled into the neighbourhood. The concert had begun. However, once in view of the venue, they saw the entry gates were still jammed with people.

"Looks like we have a problem," said Micah in a singsong voice.

Andrew flashed his volunteer badge as he and Micah passed through the disgruntled crowd. The entry was closed and the volunteers were explaining through the grills that, for safety reasons, no more people were allowed in the stadium.

"But we have tickets," pleaded one chaperone, fanning them out and holding them high. "Our group signed up early!"

Seeing Andrew's badge, a volunteer opened the gate for him and Micah, causing some of the nearby participants to mutter in discontent. Just within the gate, Andrew saw Zack.

"How did you get untethered from the computers?" jested Andrew.

Andrew introduced Micah and then asked, "What's going on?"

Zack motioned for the two to follow him as he walked away from the gate toward a large atrium pulsating with music. "Don't ask me what happened," he said, raising his voice to be heard. "Andrew, you know the opening concert is one of the biggest of the festival but the stadium can only hold about ninety thousand."

"Right. The first ninety thousand to register were supposed to get tickets," said Andrew.

"So either too many tickets were printed or a lot of people were let in the back door," injected Micah, shaking his head.

"Judging by the size of the crowds at the gates, too many tickets," said Zack.

"But that guy, right there at the gate, has a wad of tickets for his group," said Andrew. "Can't someone just check to see who's sitting in their seats?"

"The tickets are only stamped with gate and section. After that, first come, first served."

"This keeps getting better and better," quipped Micah.

"So what's going to happen?"

"Well . . . they can't come in here," said Zack. "But there are all kinds of secondary concerts going on in the city. The musicians aren't well-known but . . ."

"Emerging artists, I believe they've been called," said Andrew.

"So from the stadium to a church hall; Christian A-list bands to . . ." laughed Micah.

"The A-list 'emerged' at one time," gibed Andrew. Then looking over at the people behind the gate, "God, look at how disappointed they are."

"Some of those people had been waiting in line three hours before we opened the gates," said Zack.

"Sacrifice is part of the package," parroted Micah in a high-pitched voice.

Andrew punched Micah and the two began to walk back toward the gate.

Zack followed, baffled. "If you want, you can be crowd-control volunteers and watch from the aisles."

"Doesn't seem fair," said Andrew as they continued to walk.

"No, *we're* going to check out the *emerging* artists," said Micah.

The two were let out of the gate.

"Hey, guys," said Andrew to the people around him, "We can stay out here all night but we're not getting in. We might as well go check out some of these other musicians in the program."

As they walked back through the crowd, they repeated the message. Most turned away from the gate, weary and irritated, wandering off in different directions as they headed to other venues.

"Do you really want to check out another band?" asked Micah.

"If you want to," said Andrew. "I'd rather head back to the residence, shower and sink into my mattress."

"I'm with you."

CHAPTER 39

Day two of the festival was spread throughout the city with participants headed to venues determined by language groups. The largest, an arena that could hold thirty thousand, was allotted to the English-speaking. Each location followed the same program. The morning: skits and vignettes illustrating a particular Church teaching or Christian morals as young people sauntered in from their long commutes. At noon: a solemn liturgy celebrated with bishops and dozens of priests. Beginning in mid-afternoon: live music interspersed with motivational talks and testimonials. The evening concluded with prayer and adoration.

Andrew and Micah walked into the IFYA main site at seven thirty in the morning, muscles aching from cleaning and traipsing through the heat the day before.

"We're going to send you boys to the arena," said the director of registrations. "There's a van leaving now."

When Andrew and Micah arrived, they were directed to an office where an assistant to the events director instructed them, "You have no assigned area. You are to circulate constantly. Check the staircases, entrances, and bathrooms. Give a hand wherever necessary." They were both given walkie-talkies to alert the assistant regarding dwindling supplies, snags and emergencies, and to be called by the assistant at any moment to support as needed.

By mid-afternoon, they had notified maintenance about clogged toilets; assisted weary, light-headed teens to the medical team; moved smokers out of the stairways; and ushered bishops dropped off at the wrong entrance into their well-appointed green room to prepare for the Celebration of the Liturgy. There were no lines for food since a large service area downstairs, secured for their backpacks and stocked with water, was also used to distribute lunch and supper packs to the volunteers.

"My God, compared to yesterday, this is a cakewalk," said Micah as he sat in the air-conditioned arena to enjoy his lunch.

"Yeah, it's actually been fun getting to meet some of the people here," said Andrew sitting next to him.

"The air-conditioning helps."

~

The musicians were tuning up their instruments as the participants who had left during the extended lunch break began to pour back into the seats. Andrew and Micah were up and about making their rounds and responding to requests. The band had finished a round of Praise and Worship hymns and a young man was beginning a presentation when they re-entered the arena.

"Let's hear it for the bishops and priests!" he shouted enthusiastically. The crowd roared. "And for all who will become priests! Stand up, stand up!" Again the crowd cheered. "Let's hear it for the nuns—so many here today! Don't be shy! Stand up!" More cheers. "And all who will become nuns! Up! Up!" Clapping, hooting. "And let's hear it for our parents and all of us who will marry and raise children!" Again wild cheering. The young man held out his arms to silence the crowd, then pulled up a guitar from the nearby stand and began to strum. The crowd hushed.

"I'm here to talk about the sanctity of marriage and the sacredness of the family."

Andrew's walkie-talkie buzzed. "Just stay," he said to Micah. "If I need you, I'll come back." Then he walked out to the atrium to take the call. Thirty minutes later, he returned. "Did I miss anything?" he asked.

"Nothing you'd want to hear. This guy's a total blowhard."

"And now," said the speaker, "I want to introduce my fiancée." He waved to the wings of the stage and a young woman shyly walked to the center stage. The throng cheered, whistled and clapped.

"Shit!" said Micah, pointing to the jumbotron, "That's Mei-Lien!"

"It can't be!" exclaimed Andrew.

But as the camera zoomed in for a close-up, there was no denying it. Mei-Lien was holding hands with the presenter peering timidly at his face or down toward the floor.

"And our first kiss will be on our wedding night!" Thunderous applause. "God bless you all." He grasped his guitar in one hand, held onto Mei-Lien's with the other and walked off stage. The band began a popular Praise and Worship tune. The crowd clapped in unison and joined in the singing as the words scrolled on the monitor.

"Holy shit!" exclaimed Micah. Then looking at Andrew, he said, "Let's go make our rounds."

~

Andrew had long since given up hope of being reunited with Mei-Lien. After he'd received her letters three years ago, he held out for a few months, thinking she would change her mind. But with time, he told himself she was gone.

Over the past years he had dated a few girls, but he'd been too busy with school and work—and too poor—to pursue a relationship. A glimmer of hope sparked with the apology of Mrs. Zhang . . . No, not hope, but a whiff of feasibility. He'd been hurt too much to hope. Just the same, he was stunned by the announcement.

Mei-Lien engaged? Before finishing her graduate studies? What had happened to her dream of becoming a doctor, helping women and children?

Andrew silently made the rounds with Micah. They were going down one of the stairways when Andrew noticed Micah eyeing him with concern.

"Andrew," said Micah, "can you imagine Mrs. Zhang's reaction when *she* found out the news?" And he let out a screech that reverberated up and down the stairwell.

Andrew burst out laughing, shaking his head; then he crumpled on the steps and sobbed.

~

That evening the arena was dimmed and silent. A single spotlight shone on an elevated monstrance. Thousands of young people bowed their heads in quiet contemplation. Andrew sat among them, still dazed from the revelation of the afternoon. Micah had confiscated his walkie-talkie and left him to be undisturbed in the privacy of his thoughts. As much as Andrew had conceded that he would never be reunited with Mei-Lien, his reaction this afternoon told him that deep down, he believed there was still a possibility. He sat, stripped of his last shred of hope, in the presence of God he believed was Love.

Upset by the rigidity, monitoring, and manipulation he had encountered among the FonS members, and intrigued by the questions posed by Hachette, Andrew had gone regularly to the crusty, perceptive priest to sort through his beliefs. Over the past few years Andrew realized that, for him, the meaning of life and his experience of God was summed up in a verse from the Bible that said God is Love and anyone who lives in this Love, lives in God. It was that simple. Anything that brought him closer to Love, he accepted. The rest he left by the wayside.

But this was different. How do you let go and move on when someone you love is caught up in a mind-numbing, autocratic, Christ-proclaiming Movement, one that beguiles ardent young people like those surrounding him. And one lauded by the Pope, no less. Who was the God Mei-Lien felt compelled to follow? And how had he been drawn to a more encompassing, merciful awareness of God? Andrew stared at his hands folded on his lap. He had no answers. For some time he remained there, silent and still, no longer raking over his bewilderment and sorrow. He had no control over Mei-Lien's life; he could only embrace her with compassion. He opened his palms and let her go.

CHAPTER 40

Mrs. Zhang sat at her kitchen table staring out the window, insensible to the flowering shrubs and the chirping humming birds hovering around the feeder in the mid-July sun. Mr. Zhang sat across from her, Mei-Lien's letter open between them. Minutes passed before Mr. Zhang ventured, "It could be worse. At least she is marrying into a good family."

"Good family? Or wealthy family?" said Mrs. Zhang in a constrained, low voice.

"I imagine, both," said Mr. Zhang calmly.

"You imagine . . . And what about her education?" she said, her voice rising. "What is she going to do with a pre-med degree?"

"She might continue . . . or go into another pro—"

"Would you be so complacent if Mei-Lien was a son?" Mrs. Zhang exploded. The words flew out before she could stop them. She watched the hurt etch in his face as her accusation registered.

"No, I wouldn't be," he said, quietly. "How would he provide for a family?"

"Mei-Lien has *just* as much right to become a doctor as a son!" said Mrs. Zhang.

"But she's chosen not to."

"Chosen?" she exclaimed.

Mr. Zhang lifted up the letter. "It appears so."

Mrs. Zhang dropped her head in her hands.

"I don't love Mei-Lien any less because she is a girl," he said quietly.

"I'm so sorry . . . I'm just upset . . . so disappointed myself. I shouldn't lash out at you." Tears filled her eyes, so rare an occurrence that the affront Mr. Zhang had just experienced subsided. He reached across the table and took her hand.

"It's decided," he said. "There's nothing we can do about it."

He was right. There was nothing they could do to change their daughter's mind. Her engagement to Scott Tan had been announced. In her letter Mei-Lien quoted the Guardians who called the match "providential, designed by God Himself." She and Scott had received the vocation of Christian matrimony and would strive to be exemplars of God's vision for the family.

The wedding date, Mei-Lien wrote, was set for October on the anniversary of the founding of the PoCs. It would take place in the chapel of the Lantana residence and the reception in their dining hall. The Zhangs had only to arrive as the guests of honour.

Enraged and devastated, Mrs. Zhang felt her daughter slipping away, never to return.

CHAPTER 41

Over three hundred bishops processed out of one of the arena's side doors into the waiting motor coaches. Andrew and Micah watched as they stood in front of a metal barrier, making sure that no participants used that exit until all the bishops had boarded the buses. A gathering of young people and nuns waved and cheered as the bishops passed by and the bishops smiled and waved in return.

This had been the final prayer service, one for bishops, priests, nuns and a select number of youths. This evening would be the much anticipated evening prayer service and massive concert held for all participants. The climactic conclusion would be the Mass with the Pope tomorrow morning.

Theo, talking animatedly with one of the bishops, nearly collided with Andrew and Micah. "Oh, sorry," he exclaimed as the bishop walked on, "I didn't see you there."

"Where are the bishops off to now?" queried Micah.

"For a lunch at the Rippling Creek resort before the big day tomorrow. I'm guiding one of the buses." Then as he ran off, "See you later."

"That guy always manages to be in the thick of things!" said Micah, shaking his head.

"The 'upper' thick of things," said Andrew.

"How does he do it?"

"Or, more to the point, why does he do it?" responded Andrew.

The buses departed and Andrew and Micah pulled back the barrier to allow access to the exit doors.

"Our bus will be leaving soon," said Andrew. "We'd better pick up our meal boxes and back packs."

~

Andrew stepped out of the aging school bus onto the dry, crunching grass. Micah followed, pulling down his baseball cap to shield his eyes from the blazing sun. Grasshoppers jumped about frenetically, disturbed by the onslaught. Hundreds of volunteers had been brought to the evening concert site: a wide-open field on the outskirts of the city. For a handsome fee, the owner had allowed the field to go fallow for the concluding celebrations. Rough and clod-filled, some volunteers stumbled before acclimating to the rough terrain. They had been bussed in ahead of the participants who were arriving on foot after a nine-mile hike from the city—hundreds of thousands, packed for an over-night stay.

From the entry gate, it took forty-five minutes for Andrew and Micah to traverse the tamped down lanes and reach their section, a five-acre swath of land enclosed by fences and metal barriers. A sign high on a post declare it E-10. Arriving with them was a team of volunteers. These volunteers were to check passes and secure the section. Andrew and Micah were free-flowing agents, trouble-shooting and on call for anything out of the ordinary. Andrew gazed about. As far as he could see in every direction were fences, barriers, occasional tents, and poles bearing lights and section signs. An army of volunteers streamed through the temporary roadways, headed to their assignments. Far off, a mere blip in the flat expanse, was the stage on which the concert and Mass would take place.

Sweat emitted from their every pore. The only shade in the vast, flat expanse was that afforded by monitors and speakers dotting the field at regular intervals.

"Four hundred thousand people are spending the night in this?" exclaimed Micah. "And I thought that stuffy, old gym was bad."

"This is unbelievable," muttered Andrew. "And we were bussed here—imagine walking in this heat!

One of the volunteers standing nearby said, "This is a pilgrimage and that means sacrifice is part of it."

"Yeah, well it's one thing to face difficulties that come our way and deal with them," said Andrew. "It's another thing to concoct an inhumane environment and invite people to partake, waving off dehydration, exhaustion, sun stroke . . . and filth as an opportunity to sacrifice," said Andrew.

"This is . . . religious S&M!" said Micah.

"What do you mean?" said the volunteer warily.

"It's like baptising masochism," said Andrew.

The volunteer moved closer to her friends leaving Andrew and Micah by themselves.

"We might as well check out the territory before the participants arrive," said Micah. "I'd rather die moving than shrivel up in section E-10."

It took them twenty minutes to walk to the bevy of port-a-potties at the periphery of the field. Hand-washing stations and drinking water spigots were another few minutes away. Andrew and Micah took advantage of the primitive facilities, soaking their tee shirts, splashing water over their faces and refilling their depleted water bottles. Nothing could have prepared them for the intensity of the heat, thick with humidity, which enveloped their bodies and smoldered under their feet.

Their walkie-talkies crackled simultaneously. They were needed back at E-10.

CHAPTER 42

The sun was setting and still the participants poured into the immense field. Bedraggled, thirsty, dusty and sweaty, the participants slogged through the lanes and into their sections like refugees. E-10, as all the other sections, was packed solid with people. Early arrivals had spread out their tarps and mats to ward off the newcomers: other members of their group would be arriving soon, they said. But as time went on, even these squatters could see it was useless to resist and, willingly or begrudgingly, retracted their settlement.

Some arrivals plopped down on the uneven earth, their bare legs scratched by the dry, battened down over-growth, heads resting on their arms, oblivious to the insects jumping and crawling around them. Others dropped their backpacks and plodded to the port-a-potties and the promise of water. Still others, deriving a second wind from arriving, chatted and sang as they tried to make their spot more liveable. Chaperones gathered meal tickets from the participants in their care in order to retrieve their meal packets from various outlets around the peripheries—an errand that could take more than two hours. Andrew and Micah were kept busy answering questions, giving directions, calling First Aid, and resolving territorial disputes.

Looking at the amassing throng and the conditions they were expected to live in shocked both Andrew and Micah alike.

"This is insanity," said Andrew after he had returned from eking out a patch of dirt for a new group.

"I'm drained from just standing in the sun all day," said Micah. "These poor guys walked nine miles to get here!"

One couple, chaperoning a group from their parish, approached Andrew. "Where's the main stage we've heard so much about?" they asked, gazing to the left and right. Andrew pointed to the small, white bump on the horizon.

"That's where the Pope is going to be?" the wife exclaimed. "This was going to be the highlight—seeing the Pope! We can barely make out the stage!"

"To be honest, I can't believe it myself," said Andrew. "If it's any consolation, the concert and concluding Mass will be projected on the monitors." Andrew waved his hands toward a nearby jumbotron.

"We could have stayed home and watched the same thing on TV," said the man wearily.

"And missed all this?" said Micah, wiping off several ants crawling up his leg.

Despite their disappointment, the couple laughed. "I just hope our gang holds out. That walk nearly did them in."

"Make sure they're drinking water," said Andrew. "There are spigots near the port-a-potties. In fact, Micah and I were just headed there to fill up the bottles of some of the volunteers."

"Give me a few minutes to gather up their bottles," said the man, "and I'll go with you." He and his wife began the tedious walk back to their "camp," stepping over arms and legs and skirting primitive tents made from tarps and tee shirts.

"Few minutes?" said Micah with a smirk.

It was almost a half-hour before the man reappeared with a backpack of empty bottles.

CHAPTER 43

Andrew clicked on his walkie-talkie. "We've got a problem here." The port-a-potties were mobbed and the water dispensing area had lines that extended into the lanes dividing the sections. After squeezing through the massive pile up, Andrew and Micah finally came to the source of the problem. With the spigots fully opened, the water flowed out in little more than a trickle. With one hand, the participants were drinking out of the bottle they just replenished and with the other hand, filling up another bottle. If they came in a group, replenished bottles were past around, drunk, and replenished again. Those waiting behind urged them with growing impatience to move on. Worst were the participants who shoved from behind, forcing themselves in front of those who had already waited in line over an hour.

"We know about it," came the crackling response. "The demand is so high, the water pressure dropped. We're working on it. If everyone turned off the spigots for an hour, it would help."

"Help who?" yelled Andrew. He shook his head and rolled his eyes at Micah who could hear the conversation. "Have you been out in this desert? These people need water and *need it now*!"

"We hear you, we hear you. We're working on it."

"Well, work faster!"

Andrew and Micah arrived back at section E-10 and handed the empty water bottles to a group of disappointed volunteers. By now, the sun was dipping into the horizon. The monitors flickered on and an exuberant voice announced the beginning of the prayer service to be followed by the much-anticipated concert. "And for all you thirsty participants, we hope to have the water pressure restored shortly, so hang in there." A roar of approval rose from the crowd. "Now, let's open our prayer service with hymns of praise!"

An orchestra burst forth. Members of the choir, projected on the monitor, roused the weary crowd with rhythmic clapping. And then spirited, harmonious singing burst from the speakers.

"What the hell?" said Micah as he and Andrew scanned the crowd.

Whether it was the promise of water, or relief from the searing heat of the sun, or the vibrancy of the music, or the sunset casting its calming hues of pinks, blues and violets over the massive gathering; whatever the motive, the multitude of youth seemed to shake off their lethargy. They rose from dozing on their mats, straightened from slouching and leaning against their friends, stretched and quickened their pace as they walked back from the toilets.

"My God," said Andrew, "it's like watching the rising from the dead!"

But the momentum was short-lived. The singing subsided after several songs and the service began. The drone of prayers and the lengthy sermon soon became background noise to conversations, eating and bartering items from the meal packets, rearranging tarps and mats to deal with the pesky insects, and the unending traipsing back and forth to the port-a-potties. Occasionally, the few who were intent to listen would shush their neighbours but it was futile. Midway through the sermon a notable wave rippled through the vast mob as word spread that water had been restored.

Micah nudged Andrew to look at the jumbotron as the camera swept the crowd near the altar. The majority were sitting in rapt attention as the bishop continued with his sermon.

"Too bad there are no cameras back here to pan the crowd," said Andrew.

"Yeah," said Micah. "A shift from the pious zone to the survival zone."

CHAPTER 44

Splat . . . splat . . . splat. Andrew awoke with a start that jostled Micah, asleep nearby. Splat, splat, splat, splat. The fat drops began to fall in rapid succession awakening the mob who, wrenched from the stupor of sleep, tried to make sense of the situation. Participants clambered out of sleeping bags and huddled next to others who had turned their mats and tarps into primitive tents.

"Shit." Andrew looked at his watch. Five thirty. He and Micah jumped up, put on their backpacks and pulled down the lip of their ball caps to keep the rain off their faces.

The grooves and hollows of the fallowed fields turned to rivulets. Water pooled around the sitting participants. People jumped up, grabbing their belongings in an attempt to keep them dry or at least not muddy.

The rain subsided after about a half-hour. Some wiped-out individuals laid down their mats in the mud and slept on top of their damp sleeping bags. Most did not. Heading to the port-a-potties, they poured out of their sections into the lanes, churning the packed, drenched dirt into a mud slick.

∼

Andrew and Micah were no longer on duty. They had handed in their walkie-talkies sometime after midnight and debated whether to walk back to the city or remain on site for the next day's festivities. Exhausted, the thought of a nine-mile walk in the middle of the night induced them to hunker down near a fence post in their section and try to get some sleep. Andrew heard Micah's deep breathing around two and drifted off some time after that.

Since neither had anything to protect them from the rain other than a light windbreaker, they set off for the toilets while the rain was still pouring and arrived as the cloud burst was drizzling to a close. Just the same, by the time they reached the port-a-potties, the lines were excessive.

Mud oozing through and around their sandals, Andrew and Micah stood gridlocked for fifteen minutes as participants surged into the area. The lines disappeared and became a shambling hoard inching closer and closer to the row of port-a-potties.

"This is crap," said Andrew, moving away from the pileup.

"Literally," said Micah.

They squeezed their way out of the crowd and walked beyond the port-a-potties until they were on the outskirts of the field near the security fences. Though the ground was wet, the scorched grassy clumps were still intact, so the young men were no longer walking in mud. On they walked until they were behind another row of toilets. Protected from view, they walked to the fence and fertilized the field beyond.

Zipping up, Andrew looked across the open field and watched the rain clouds sailing away.

"Would you believe that?" said Micah as he turned and gazed at the sun cresting above the horizon. "We get enough rain to deprive us of sleep and now we're in for another blazing day."

"With humidity to boot!" said Andrew.

The two walked on toward the stage, avoiding the crowds by skirting the fence. Eventually they came to a large medical tent. They sat in its shade on their wind breakers and finished off what remained in their food packs.

"So what do you want to do?" asked Andrew. "We could head back to town now or wait for the Pope and the concluding Mass."

"The Pope will be here in about an hour. Why not wait? I mean, things can only go up from here!" said Micah, laughing.

They decided to get as close to the front as possible. However, before long they were blocked from skirting the edge of the field by security fences that cut in front of their path and forced them to the crowded lanes between the sections. Constrained to stop by congestion from an intercepting lane, Andrew and Micah watched participants consolidate their belongings from their overnight stay.

"I'm not hauling out this sleeping bag," said one.

"Oh, you don't have to," said another. "I heard if we leave things we don't want, they'll be given to the homeless. You can leave your stool and tarp—your mat, too."

Micah's eyes popped wide in surprise while Andrew laughed in disbelief.

"The homeless?" Andrew said over the fence. "The homeless want these trodden down mats and tarps? These soggy, muddy sleeping bags?"

The group on the other side of the fence stared at the eavesdroppers. "I'm *sure* those collecting these things are going to wash them," said one.

"Why don't *you* bring them home and wash them! *I'm* sure anything left here is going into a landfill," said Micah as he moved ahead.

As they walked further on, Andrew and Micah discovered the reason for the congestion. The lanes going down toward the stage were blocked and participants were told to go back to their sections. No one would be allowed to loiter in the lanes for safety reasons. As Andrew approached, he held up his volunteer badge. With his upgraded clearance, he and Micah were allowed to go through.

On they trod toward the main stage until about three blocks away, it loomed before them in all its immensity. Rather than the crowded, mucky sections behind them, the sections in front of the stage were populated with orderly rows of chairs that were quickly filling with robed clergy. Row upon row, a sea of white.

"This is odd," quipped Micah. "I thought this festival was for young people." He looked back. "The sections with the mobs of youth who have been out here all night don't even begin before . . . How far back do you think they are?"

Andrew looked back to the first section and drew his gaze across the field of priests to the stage. "A quarter of a mile?"

"Why aren't the priests in the back and the kids in the front? Seems a little backward."

They were now at the huge expanse between the first row of seats and the stage. To the side of the clergy, about twenty rows deep, were chairs filled with suited men, well-dressed women and starched children.

"They obviously did not spend the night under the stars," said Micah. Next to the occupants of this gated community, they realized just how dishevelled they looked: from their sweat-streaked bodies and dusty clothes down to their mud-packed feet.

"Excuse me, excuse me," shouted someone from the side wing. "No one is allowed . . . Oh, it's you, Andrew!" said Theo, approaching the two. He, too, was dressed in a suit, his shoes polished, his hair neatly combed. "What are you doing up here?"

"We've been in the back sections since yesterday," said Andrew. "We thought we'd come to see what's going on up here, maybe see the Pope."

"Ah, well," said Theo nervously, pulling the two aside, "you see . . . you can't really be up here. This section is reserved for the clergy and dignitaries."

"Oh, the dignitaries!" said Micah, raising his eyebrow, "as different from the what . . . the thousands upon thousands of young people who trudged through the heat yesterday, spent the night in the dirt, and are currently piled up at the toilets so they can piss? They're a mile and more away from the stage making way for the—"

A golf cart loaded with cases of bottled water made its way up a switchback ramp to the plateau of the stage. Micah and Andrew swung their heads to the area from which the golf cart came. Under the shade of a lean-to were pallets of bottled water.

"Who is that water for?" asked Andrew.

"We have volunteers who will be distributing it to the bishops and dignitaries. It can get very warm on the stage."

"On the stage?" said Andrew. "Just a heads up, it's a desert out on those fields and we sure could have used this water yesterday when the tap dried out."

"It would never have been enough for everyone," said Theo, his irritation rising.

"It would have been something," said Micah.

A voice on the loud speaker boomed out, "The Pope's helicopter is approaching! He'll soon be landing!"

Cheers resounded.

"You have to leave," said Theo urgently. "You don't have clearance. I don't know how you passed through security. I could call in a golf—"

"We're leaving, Theo, we're leaving," said Andrew as he and Micah turned back toward the lane.

CHAPTER 45

Under the unrelenting sun the lanes between the sections had dried and were being ground to dust by the thousands who tramped over them. Little clouds arose with each footfall and swirls of fine particles gusted through the participants when the Pope's helicopter hovered over the crowd before landing. Andrew and Micah shielded their eyes and pulled up their t-shirts to cover their nose and mouth. By the time they neared E-10 the Pope was on the stage and beginning the celebration of the Mass. They paused to observe the opening rites but, exhausted and disillusioned, neither had the desire to remain. They walked back toward the peripheries in order to use the toilets, fill up their water bottles and leave the grounds.

The swarming mass at the port-a-potties was larger than the morning crowd. Some women were hunched over in pain as they waited their turn.

"This is ridiculous," said Andrew. He and Micah walked through the crowd, encouraging the men to go to the fence and leave the stalls to the women. The word spread. Men left the lines, easing the demand for the port-a-potties. Initially, the volunteers on duty called the men back, but their orders were ignored and more men joined their ranks. After relieving themselves, Micah said to Andrew, "Well, the grass will be greener on the other side of this fence!"

They were approaching the rear sections when a man, noticing their volunteer badges, ran up to them.

"I can't find my daughter," he said frantically pointing to the large medical tent nearby. "She collapsed and they brought her here, but now I can't find her!"

"There must be a misunderstanding," said Andrew. He introduced himself and Micah and they began to walk with the man back to the medical tent. "She's sixteen . . . It's so God damn hot . . . We've been telling the kids to drink water but the toilets are so crowded and dirty, they don't want to . . . She fainted . . . We brought her here."

"We're going to help you find your daughter. What's her name?"

"Jenny . . . Jennifer Harvey."

The entrance to the medical tent was inundated with people seeking assistance. One staff circulated among the waiting crowd as a pre-triage, ushering the most urgent to the front of the line to be assessed by the triage nurses.

"The staff brought my daughter to an examination room and told me to go to an entrance in the back . . . but they can't find her!"

"Let's go to the back. We'll find her."

Andrew flashed his badge and explained the situation to the security guard at the back entrance and they were allowed to enter. Andrew was floored by the sight. The space was the size of a school gym. Hundreds of patients lay in rows, one next to the other. Poles stood at intervals along the rows, holding up ropes and off the ropes hung intravenous bags with tubes dangling to the arms of the patients.

"Dehydration, heat exhaustion," whispered the security guard. "You should see the auxiliary tent behind this one. They put it up last night. It's filled with dehydrated kids who haven't reached this stage," he said as he swept out his arm toward the scene. "The staff is plying them with water."

An ambulance pulled up to the back entrance and two paramedics entered the tent with a stretcher. The security guard blocked Andrew and his group from further access. "We have to wait until the paramedics are gone."

A nurse indicated a youth. The paramedics carefully transferred the patient to the stretcher. As they approached the back entrance, the father lunged forward, "Jenny, Jenny!" The security guard held him back until the father saw that the patient was a young man and fell back.

The nurse, overwhelmed by the sheer numbers under her care, allowed the father to walk through the rows provided he was accompanied by Andrew and Micah. Patient by patient, the father scrutinized the faces. As each row was examined, Andrew noted the growing anxiety of the father. "If we don't find Jenny soon, we may have a cardiac arrest on our hands," whispered Micah.

They were nearing the end of the final row and Jenny's father was trembling.

"There are more patients in the tent next door," said Andrew. "Jenny must be there."

"There's another tent?" he asked, a ray of hope returning to his harried eyes.

Inside the second tent, hundreds of young people sat cross-legged or lay down, water bottles in hand. Here volunteers were assisting a nurse, handing out water and encouraging the dehydrated to drink. Jenny was spotted in a corner, her back resting against the side of the tent. When she saw her father, she began to weep and when he knelt beside her, she wound her arms around his neck. "I just want to go home," she cried. An adhesive bandage on her forearm showed that she had been hydrated intravenously and then transferred to the auxiliary tent to make way for new arrivals and complete her recovery.

Supporting her around the waist, the dad brought Jenny to a standing position and walked her to the exit. The nurse approached them.

"I would advise you to stay a little longer before going back to the field," she said.

"The FIELD?" he yelled. "There's no f—king way my daughter is going back into that desert! We need to get to the city. Now!"

"I'm sorry, but we don't have any transportation for that," said the nurse meekly.

"Well, someone better provide it because there is no way my daughter is going to walk nine god-damn miles back to the city in her condition!"

Andrew could see that the nurse, though empathizing with Jenny and her father, had no means of responding to the request.

"I think we can work this out," he told the nurse, who returned to her duties.

"Stay here a few minutes and Micah and I will find a ride for you."

After they left the tent Micah said, "And how are we going to perform this miracle, Jesus?"

"Let's see if the security guard we met at the first tent has any connections," said Andrew as they walked toward the adjacent medical tent.

When the security guard saw them again he asked, "Did he find his daughter?"

"Yes," said Andrew, "but we have another problem." Andrew briefed him on the situation.

"What a screwup! I hope the organizers have buses lined up for these guys," indicating the rows of patients. "There is no way they are walking out of here." Then turning back to Andrew and Micah, "My shift ends soon and I have a replacement coming in. I'll radio in and see if we can squeeze a couple more people in our vehicle."

Fifteen minutes later, a jeep pulled up and four security guards piled out, replacing those at the medical tents. Jenny and her dad were loaded in with the guards who had been relieved and departed in a cloud of dust.

CHAPTER 46

"That was exhausting . . . and we don't even know Jenny!" said Micah.

"It's insane," said Andrew.

The two turned and walked back to the main lane that would take them to the exit. Harmonious voices and music from the orchestra blared from the speakers. Andrew and Micah turned to a nearby monitor towering above them, high in the scaffolds. The Pope, accompanied by deacons and assistants in ceremonial vestments, walked solemnly around the altar, incense bellowing from the thurible he gently swung.

Below the monitor, scores of participants were packing up what they needed for the hike back to the city and leaving the rest behind. Packaged sandwiches, cookies and other snacks spilled out of discarded meal packs and baked on the dusty field. Empty water bottles and plastic bags rolled and twirled in the wake of the departing participants. And as the retreating plodded past the barricades to their sections, now wide open, they joined the steady stream of people who were already on the lanes leaving the site. The closer Andrew and Micah got to the exit, the larger the exodus from the fenced sections.

On the nine-mile trek back, neither said a word. On they trudged following the designated route into the city, grateful to the homeowners who, holding lawn hoses, sprayed them with water and allowed them to fill their water bottles. City buses, anticipating the exodus, lined the street near the first stop. Andrew and Micah climbed aboard with a host of other dishevelled participants and forced themselves to stay awake so as not to miss their stop.

CHAPTER 47

Micah outright refused to dislodge himself from bed, so Andrew made his way to the IFYA offices alone. Having spent nine months as a long-term volunteer, Andrew returned one last time to debrief. As he entered the building, he shivered from the blast of icy air-conditioning. Jubilation flowed out of the offices and down the corridor in animated anecdotes, resounding laughter, high-fives, hugs and some tears of joy. Dispirited and drained Andrew felt he was in an alternate reality.

As he made his way to the executive director's office a couple of staff members walking down the hall greeted him warmly and slapped him affectionately on the shoulder. The director's door was ajar. Andrew knocked and opened it wider. No one was there.

"Go on in," said a jovial voice. Theo stood directly behind him carrying a plate laden with breakfast food. Andrew stepped into the office to allow Theo to enter. "Breakfast is being served in the conference room. Go grab a plate. There's plenty! Compliments of the director!" Theo settled into a cushioned chair facing the desk.

"Is Fr. Steve in?" asked Andrew.

"No, 'il direttore' hasn't arrived yet," said Theo, digging into his meal.

"Il direttore?"

Theo laughed, "That's what the Pope calls him, 'il direttore esecutivo'!"

"When do you expect him in?" asked Andrew wearily.

"Don't know. Maybe an hour or so?" Theo continued eating. "He's held up somewhere. Sure you don't want something to eat?"

"I just came by to sign off and bring up a few concerns."

"Fr. Steve has a packed schedule this week: debriefings, closing down the sites . . . Oh, and he's meeting with some bishops from overseas before they head back. It just goes on and on."

A head popped in the door. "Okay, it's set up, Theo. Tell Fr. Steve when he comes in that the sandwiches are being dropped off at the homeless shelter—all ten thousand of them."

"Will do!" Theo set down his plate and grabbed a pad of paper and pen from the desk.

"Ten thousand sandwiches?" repeated Andrew.

"More or less. You know, the good ones—subs. The homeless will love them."

"How old are they?"

"I don't know. They were made for the Saturday lunch but somehow these didn't get picked up. The participants must have eaten elsewhere. Well, I guess it's better to have too much than too little!" laughed Theo as he finished his notation. "They'll be put to good use now."

"If they're any good to use. What a waste."

Theo seemed not to hear. As he resumed his breakfast he said, "Can you believe it! We estimate nine hundred thousand were at the final Mass! The biggest gathering yet! It was amazing to see!"

"I guess that depends on what you saw."

"The Pope was elated and personally thanked Fr. Steve."

"The Pope didn't see what I saw or he would never be able to justify the gathering."

"What a downer."

"You weren't on the verge of dehydration for most of Saturday and Sunday. From the looks of you on Sunday, you hadn't spent the night in a bug-infested dustbowl."

Theo looked at Andrew quizzically. He seemed to have forgotten their encounter the previous day.

"You weren't caring for the thousands of sick and heat exhausted youth in the medical tents or trying to calm and connect them with distraught parents. You weren't there and neither was the Pope, or the bishops, or 'il direttore' for that matter! So instead of high-fiving each other you may want to consider the morality of encouraging hundreds of thousands of young people to massive functions that you are ill-equipped to manage."

"We know, and they know, that sacrifice is involved," said Theo, his voice rising, "and they are willing to join themselves with Christ's suffering on the—"

"Cut the sacrifice shit, Theo. There's no need to drag hundreds of thousands of young people across the world to one spot for them to experience Christ. From what I saw, most of them were too exhausted to even attend to what was going on. Is this really about the young people or is it about the power to whip up a large gathering that shouts chants to the Pope!"

"I don't have to listen to this," said Theo, standing. "What I saw and what *everyone else in this office saw* was an outpouring of faith."

"What you saw was an outpouring of trust that the chaperones and young people had in you and in the Church leaders who encouraged them to come. And when they're faced with foul-ups and disorganization, they're told it's all part of following the suffering Christ—how expedient."

"Inconveniences are a part of life," retorted Theo. "Go to any football game."

"A football game is your choice, Theo. I haven't heard of the Church passing out special indulgences for going to the Super Bowl. But that's beside the point. What I saw and experienced this weekend was way beyond inconvenient. It was dangerous, Theo. It's unethical to submit people to those conditions—for what? To meet the Pope? Participate in some mega-liturgy? Shit, they could barely see the stage let alone participate! I'm sorry I had any part in it."

Andrew walked toward the door, then stopped and turned back toward Theo, "And maybe you can jot all this down on that note pad of yours and share it with Fr. Steve."

A few moments later, Andrew walked out of the main door, leaving behind the fabricated air of the IFYA office, and embraced the oppressive heat.

PART THREE

CHAPTER 48

"What!" exclaimed Mrs. Zhang.

"You heard right, Mom." Mei-Lien sounded depressed. "Emily and Amy are going to the International Festival for Young Adults with their dad. The girls will be gone for almost two weeks; Scott a little longer—some follow up meetings with the directors and the Founder after that."

Sixteen years before, Mrs. Zhang would have flown off the handle, screeching her opposition: *He's leaving you alone! A wife, who will be seven months pregnant, in Hong Kong, away from family, with three young children! That thoughtless, self-centered* . . . But those days had long since passed.

"I'll push my trip forward, Mei-Lien. I'll be there before the girls leave."

"Thanks, Mom."

The words filled the eyes of Mrs. Zhang with tears. Mei-Lien was worn down from a difficult pregnancy. This would be her sixth child, five years after her youngest and following a miscarriage. Mei-Lien had called her mom with an unspoken request, a request Mrs. Zhang had desired for years. She wanted her mother.

"I'll see you soon, Mei-Lien."

~

Over the years Mrs. Zhang had remained on the fringes of the PoCs. She kept her attendance at meetings and retreats minimal, just enough to meet the requisites or satisfy her curiosity regarding new initiatives. She gave sparingly at collections even though tithing was upheld as the ideal. And despite the goading to increase membership, she hadn't brought one person to the PoC fold, not even her husband. She bowed her head and confessed vague or imaginary offenses during the communal "divestment," a monthly practice "to foster the recognition of one's sinfulness." She never pointed out the faults in the others, though these "fraternal elucidations" were said to be "gifts of God to strip away pride and ignorance," gifts that should be received with "profound gratitude as they fostered conversion of heart." Mrs. Zhang considered the sessions little more than pecking parties feeding the group's internal surveillance. Nothing was considered too insignificant or too intimate. Elucidations could move from an unkempt home to inquiries about birth control and sexual relations if a couple had only one or two of children.

The most common "elucidation" Mrs. Zhang received from the other members was her unexceptional involvement in the Movement. There could be no advancement toward a "greater commitment to Christ" without a "higher degree of self-sacrifice and a more ardent adherence to the statutes of the PoCs." And what about her husband? Was she not concerned about his eternal salvation? Had she not considered that her tepidity could be the reason for his lack of interest in the PoCs? During these sessions, Mrs. Zhang would listen with eyes cast down, nodding at their admonitions, maintaining her composure for the sake of her daughter.

Within a year of her marriage, Mei-Lien gave birth to her first child. During her visits, Mrs. Zhang refrained from interfering regardless of the urge. After a couple of years, she was welcomed to stay at her daughter's home for several weeks during her summer break. With each additional child, Mei-Lien appeared to be more pragmatic and less idealistic. Pious adages from the PoC Founder, supplied aplenty by coordinators for every occasion, were quoted less frequently. During Scott's diatribes to Mrs. Zhang about the dismal state of the world,

Mei-Lien would remember some household task to be done and quietly leave the room.

But when Scott volunteered their family to be itinerant missionaries in Asia—Hong Kong to be exact—Mrs. Zhang noted a marked change in her daughter. She knew Mei-Lien was concerned about Amy, her anxious, methodical second daughter. To be uprooted from all that was familiar did not seem to be in her daughter's best interest, or any of her children for that matter. The youngest of her five children was still a toddler and her oldest, Emily, just twelve.

Scott, however, was unyielding. Where was her faith? Could God not work miracles if they trusted in him? Besides, to be immersed in a different culture would only benefit the children. When Mei-Lien called her mother with the news, she brought up her concerns but, catching herself, she repeated what her PoC confessor had said: her faith was being tested like Abraham when he set out for the Promised Land.

Mrs. Zhang was visiting when the PoC national leaders came to meet with the family to finalize the decision. Mei-Lien let Scott do the talking and silently acquiesced. The family was rewarded with praise for their faith and missionary zeal and, later, with a celebration of blessings from the PoC community. Within months, the majority of their possessions were distributed or sold.

Mrs. Zhang knew all about the missionary families who sallied forth to their assignments without knowing the language of the country or its culture, and without any job security. Regardless of their own financial straits, the PoC families who remained at home were financially responsible for the missionaries' housing, food, education and other expenses. The exhortation for money was never ceasing at her PoC meetings. Scott was assured of some position in his father's business, so their family would be less of a burden.

Mrs. and Mr. Zhang were at the airport when Mei-Lien and her family boarded the plane to Rome. With a number of other families, they were scheduled for a blessing from the Pope before heading to their missionary destinations. In that final hug, Mei-Lien had clung to her mother and sobbed for a few minutes before Scott impatiently urged her to move through the security gate.

CHAPTER 49

Mei-Lien's transfer to Hong Kong had been a severe blow to Mrs. Zhang. All summer she had remained with Mei-Lien, helping her to sort, pack and manage her large family. Scott was occupied with business meetings and PoC affairs until the last couple of weeks. By then Mr. Zhang had arrived. So while the furniture was sold and towed away, and the rental agreement for their house signed, the Zhangs, Mei-Lien, and the kids played in the parks, went to the pool, and had picnics near the lake outside the city.

Back at the college, Mrs. Zhang slipped into the groove she had followed for years. She and Mr. Zhang had discussed retiring and moving closer to Mei-Lien but her move to Hong Kong stymied that idea and their retirement was put on hold. A year after Mei-Lien's departure, Mr. Zhang suffered a massive heart attack and died. With her husband buried and Mei-Lien on the other side of the world, Mrs. Zhang battled against waves of despondency.

Within her local PoC community, Mrs. Zhang's indifferent reputation had been burnished to a high sheen as the mother of a missionary family: an honour Mrs. Zhang neither sought nor valued. Underneath her unflagging demeanour, her emotions roiled with regret, doubt, rage, and depression.

~

Forced to hide her faith as a child to a young adult, Mrs. Zhang was a staunch adherent of the Catholic Church and a supporter of the underground Church in China. She had had no tolerance for those who sought a more conciliatory stance between the Church and the Chinese government nor could she stomach anyone in the US Church who appeared to weaken Church teaching or assimilate secular values. But with Mei-Lien's recruitment to the PoCs and her own experience of the Movement, Mrs. Zhang's intransigent positions began to amend.

In her years with the PoCs, she had witnessed unequivocal certainty as the gateway for unchecked power, blanket judgments, the demand for unquestioning obedience, and manipulation justified to advance God's kingdom on earth. She blamed her rigid beliefs for her controlling upbringing of Mei-Lien, but not entirely.

Born an only child after several miscarriages, Mrs. Zhang was raised by a disappointed father who had desired a son and a mother saddened she had not produced one. Her unrelenting dedication to her studies was driven by her parents' pride in her academic success. When Mei-Lien was born under similar conditions, Mrs. Zhang thought she detected the same disappointment in Mr. Zhang. In retrospect, she saw that her husband's disappointment in not having a son did not mean he considered his daughter inferior, and his hands-off approach to Mei-Lien's upbringing was a result of her own domineering character. She realized she had pressured Mei-Lien toward academic excellence because she was still desperately striving to validate her own worth.

Coupled with these mortifying insights was her bewilderment over the Pope's unilateral approval for Movements like the PoCs. The PoC Founder and his immediate associates were often pictured with the Pope, either piously praying at a private Mass or smiling broadly while presenting some publication or gift: pictures that plastered the walls of PoC buildings and embellished their brochures.

Did no one investigate these organizations before approval, she wondered? Were their methods of recruitment and control ever scrutinized—not on paper but in practice? Were financial audits required? Did they question why members were encouraged to donate in cash? PoC members were never given an accounting locally or globally for the amount of funds collected or where they were distributed. How were those international study centres built and funded? How much compensation did the Founder, his associates and their families receive? And not just in funds, but also in the amount and style of their travel, in their homes at the scenic PoC centres, in the chef-prepared meals they enjoyed there, and in the tailored clothing they wore?

And did no one question the wisdom of sending young families as missionaries? The Pope often expounded on the need to support families. Yet, didn't he or the bishops realize the importance of the extended family and friends for strengthening family ties and caring for the children? Was there no consideration for the extra stress put upon these families? Did no one look beyond the complacent smiles and emotional tears during the Vatican sending-off ceremonies to unearth the struggles she had seen in her own daughter? How could they be so blind?

~

Mrs. Zhang never uttered a word about her struggles to Mei-Lien. As her attitudes shifted, Mrs. Zhang distanced herself more and more from friends and organizations that had shared her previous views. Her peace and purpose were found in doing everything she could to support her daughter. And now after sixteen years, Mei-Lien had turned to her for help.

CHAPTER 50

Mrs. Zhang had arrived a couple of days before the scheduled departure of Scott and his two daughters. The following day, however, brought about an abrupt change of plans for Scott.

A property dispute exploded in Australia and the PoC leaders needed someone with Scott's eloquence, business acumen and negotiating skills to douse the flames and resolve the dispute in the best interest of the PoCs. The Hong Kong contingent of PoC youths headed for the IFYA were placed in the hands of a Guardian, Nina, who, up to that point, had been second-in-command under Scott.

~

"You'll be with your sister from morning 'til night the entire trip, Amy. I've told you that a thousand times," said Scott as he shoved his wallet in his back pocket and picked up his keys.

Emily, his eldest child, was confident, vivacious and brilliant in languages. Amy was shy, nervous and uncomfortable in crowds. Unlike Emily, she had never been to a regional youth festival let alone the international. Scott felt this would be the perfect opportunity for her to spread her wings and "move out of her comfort zone." Mei-Lien was not so sanguine. She had been a part of the IFYA in the past and had experienced its gruelling series of events. She agreed to let her daughters go under one condition: neither Emily nor Amy would participate in the overnight festivities or the concluding Mass. They would stay at a PoC centre and watch these events on TV with the older and disabled PoC participants. After consultation with the organizers of the Hong Kong contingent, Scott confirmed that Mei-Lien's conditions were accepted.

"Amy, we'll be joined at the hips!" said Emily. "You'll see, it's going to be lots of fun."

"You promise?"

"I promise, I promise, I promise! Are you convinced now?" Amy gave a weak smile. "Come on, let's get our packs."

The girls brought their backpacks and sleeping bags to the front door of the apartment and began hugging their mother, grandma and three younger siblings.

"I want to stay home with you and Grandma," said Amy, wavering as she hugged her mother.

"Don't coddle her, Mei-Lien," said Scott as he picked up Amy's backpack and handed it to her.

"Nina told me that you and Emily would always be together. She gave me her word. You'll be home in no time at all," said Mei-Lien as she gave Amy one last hug. When Emily embraced her mom, Mei-Lien whispered, "Don't let her out of your sight." Emily kissed her mom and nodded.

"Let's go," said Scott. "We need to get to the centre to catch the bus. I don't want to be late."

Scott accompanied Nina and their team to the airport and made sure they were safely boarded before returning home. He was in the midst of a phone conversation when he returned to the apartment. He went to the couch where his ten-year-old son, John Paul, sat with a book. Scott waved to catch his attention and signalled him to read elsewhere. A flurry of other calls followed during which he constantly referred to his laptop.

Mei-Lien helped her mother prepare dinner and tried to keep the younger children, Grace, seven, and Peter, five, from under their father's feet. Occasionally, Scott would wave his hands indicating he wanted less noise. Mei-Lien would respond by pointing to their bedroom.

After a couple of hours, Scott exclaimed into the phone, "I got it . . . Let me open it . . . Yes, it's all here. Was that the last of them, Marco? Good, good . . . Yes, I'll call you from Perth . . . Yes, thanks. The same to you."

Scott closed his laptop and packed it in a travelling bag.

"Dinner's on the stove if you want to eat before you go," said Mei-Lien.

"No, I'll pick up something at the airport. I'm going to shower and then I'll be off."

Within a half-hour Scott emerged from the bedroom with the suitcase Mei-Lien had packed. His three youngest children were playing with their toys or reading a book. He ruffled their hair saying, "Be good for Mommy and Grandma." Then he kissed his wife on the forehead and gave his mother-in-law a hug.

"We've got a real problem on our hands in Australia. I wouldn't be surprised if it takes three to four weeks to sort out. I'll be in touch." Then turning to Mrs. Zhang, "I'm so glad you're here with Mei-Lien. When I told Marco—he's our regional director—when I told him you were here for an extended visit he said, 'All things work together for those who serve the Lord!' God indeed is watching over us." With that, Scott slung his travel bag over his shoulder and rolled his suitcase out the door.

CHAPTER 51

"Sweet Jesus," sighed Mei-Lien after she closed the door.

Mrs. Zhang raised an eyebrow. "John Paul, Grace and David—it's time for bed. Mei-Lien, go sit down and put your feet up."

After the children were settled, Mrs. Zhang returned to the front room with two glasses of iced tea. Mei-Lien was sitting at one end of the couch, her feet resting on an upturned laundry basket, a fan blowing her hair away from her face. She smiled when her mom handed her the chilled drink.

"Thanks. It's so hot. Even with all the windows open, it's impossible to get a cross-breeze in this apartment."

"Do you want anything to eat?"

"Are there any more of the honey roasted peanuts you brought?"

Mrs. Zhang always arrived in Hong Kong with a large suitcase filled with necessities for Mei-Lien's growing family. She learned long before that money gifts went straight to Scott. Now when she visited, she brought clothing, dry goods and treats she knew that Mei-Lien and the children enjoyed.

"Peanuts? Oh, you've only seen a sample of the stash I hustled through customs."

Mrs. Zhang went to her suitcase that was tucked in a corner of the front room and pulled out a bag of the peanuts. Mei-Lien took a handful.

"These were always my favourites."

Mrs. Zhang sat next to her daughter and sipped her tea. "What a whirlwind these two days have been."

"Scott thrives on it."

"Did you have any idea Scott would be leaving for Australia?"

"No, but I'm sure he did."

Mrs. Zhang shot a glance at Mei-Lien. Never had she been so forthcoming. "What do you mean?"

"It's a game he's been playing for some time." Mei-Lien let out a deep breath and took another handful of peanuts. "He arranges things with the directors, or with his father if it concerns the business. A day or so before everything is scheduled, he makes a grand announcement, acting like he's just found out and everything is so urgent. (Mei-Lien waved her arm frantically.) And at that point, there's no time for discussion or getting anyone else for the job."

"How did you find this out?"

"I translate documents, Mom. Several years ago, I had to summarize and translate proceedings for a particular project. From the dates and minutes of the meetings, I realized Scott was involved in planning a lengthy business trip long before it was sprung on me. He had known about the trip weeks before! When it happened again, I made innocuous comments about some aspect of the trip around the wives of the leaders. They started to chat and soon enough I find out that, again, Scott's trip had been in the works for some time. Repeat, repeat, repeat."

"You've never asked him about it?" Mrs. Zhang asked softly.

"What for?" said Mei-Lien, her voice rising. "Nothing will change. I'll just be accused of distrust and snooping around, and not only by him. After he talks around I'll be confronted during the ... *divestments*," her voice tinged with sarcasm at the word. Mei-Lien sipped from her iced tea. "Besides, it's more entertaining to watch when he thinks I don't have a clue."

Mrs. Zhang, astounded by the raw honesty and explicit disgust of her daughter, moved to the edge of the sofa and looked directly at Mei-Lien.

"Mom, I'm so screwed." Mei-Lien's face crumpled as she began to sob. Mrs. Zhang took Mei-Lien in her arms and gently rocked her. After a while, Mei-Lien began to whisper, "I don't know if I ever loved Scott... You know, I was so starry-eyed about doing God's will, about being faithful to the Pope, to the Church. And there was Scott. He believed the same things. And he had no fear getting in front of a crowd and professing his faith. He was so sure of himself and his faith ... and so engaging and interested in me. I was mesmerized."

Mrs. Zhang leaned over to a side table and passed Mei-Lien a box of tissues. After wiping her eyes and blowing her nose, Mei-Lien leaned back against her mother. "All the Guardians told me it was a match made in heaven. Mrs. Tan and Connie were thrilled to have me in the family ... I thought I was in love ... And then we were held up as the ideal couple and I believed we must be. Scott was always eager to speak at conferences and pulled me on stage with him ... and then me and the kids, as they were born.

"And the translations! My God, all the translating!" Mei-Lien winced at the thought. "From the time we were married, I became the primary translator of PoC materials into Chinese and praised among the directors for my selfless dedication. After Grace was born, I couldn't keep up. I was busy enough with four kids and all the local meetings and events of the PoCs.

"Mom, I was sent stacks of articles and booklets that the Founder wanted translated. And then Scott's family! They needed translations for their contracts and advertisements. On top of all that, there were the simultaneous translations! I don't know how I did it when I had three kids. A few times, before I clued into Scott's tactics, I was abruptly flown to international PoC gatherings for simultaneous translations. But after Grace it became overwhelming.

"I translated a few things when I felt up to it and the rest piled up. Sooner or later, I figured, they would find someone else. I started to balk when asked to pack up the kids and travel here and there for family conferences. I felt like we were just props." Some moments passed. "Scott's embarrassed by me."

"Scott's an idiot," said Mrs. Zhang.

"I'm not zealous enough—Scott being the Hong Kong coordinator and all. You know what I'm accused of during the divestments? Being too wrapped up in my kids . . . especially Amy."

Mrs. Zhang said nothing as she gently held her daughter. Her body trembled as she released pent up memories and emotions. Gradually, weariness overtook her and Mei-Lien began to nod off.

Mrs. Zhang nudged Mei-Lien to her feet. "Let's get to bed."

CHAPTER 52

The next morning Mrs. Zhang let Mei-Lien sleep in. Together with their grandma, the children made a game of tiptoeing and whispering as they got ready for the day. After breakfast they stuffed their swimming gear, towels and snacks into their backpacks. Then Mrs. Zhang walked them to a local pool for their morning day camp. She returned just as Mei-Lien waddled out of the bedroom on her way to shower.

Mrs. Zhang stripped her daughter's murphy bed, put on fresh sheets and folded the bed into the wall. The small room transformed into an office as the top of a desk, hinged to the bottom of the bed, pivoted into place. She went on to straighten up the children's room. Designed to be the master bedroom, it was somewhat larger than Mei-Lien's and Scott's. Two sets of bunk beds flanked the sidewalls, framing a rectangular window above and a dresser below. The two youngest slept together in one of the lower bunks. Mrs. Zhang had appropriated Amy's bed across from them. On the sidewalls, a narrow shelf supported by aluminum brackets ran the length of the bed for both the upper and lower bunks. Here the children arranged their toys and other possessions and, on Amy's, Mrs. Zhang had whacked her head more than once. Clothes that didn't fit in the dresser were stored in plastic containers under the lower bunks.

The bathroom and bedroom doors opened to the kitchen-front

room and when she had finished with the children's room, she began to clean this area. Mei-Lien emerged from the bathroom wrapped in a towel and re-entered her room to get dressed.

"Thanks, Mom, for making the bed."

When the door closed, Mrs. Zhang hastened to wipe down the dining room table and fold it, like the murphy bed, into the wall. The few folding chairs she and the children had used, she returned to the small storage closet near the front door. Mrs. Zhang was sweeping the floor when Mei-Lien came out of her room. She hugged her mother as she whispered, "You have no idea how much I appreciate this."

Mrs. Zhang was uncertain if the confidence shared the night before would continue. Would Mei-Lien be ashamed of what she disclosed in a moment of exhaustion and revert back to her cryptic communication? She decided to give Mei-Lien an opening. After settling her on the sofa with her breakfast, Mrs. Zhang said, "It's amazing how you cope in such tight quarters."

"I don't," was her blunt reply. "We're crawling all over each other. If the kids didn't go to school, we'd all go crazy."

"Is there a chance of getting a bigger place?"

"Mom, this apartment is considered palatial for the average family. Scott's parents are paying for it."

"That's generous."

"Yes, that's what Scott would like me to believe." Mei-Lien shot a glance at her mother and shook her head. "Mr. Tan wanted Scott in Hong Kong for his business. Coupling the transfer with a missionary assignment simply gilded the undertaking. I'm sure our rent is some kind of payment for services rendered."

"Do you see much of the Tans?"

"They drop in when they're travelling to Singapore. Mrs. Tan offered to get me someone to help around the house, but I turned her down."

"Why?" asked Mrs. Zhang, surprised.

"Because I know who I'd get. Do you remember the women who cleaned and cooked when I was at the Lantana residence?"

"Yes."

"Well, they're called Assistants—helpers for the Guardians. Most of them have escaped from impoverished or abusive situations in other countries. They don't marry and spend their lives cooking and cleaning at the various PoC institutions. I've never known one to be offered an education or move out on her own. They are completely dependent on the PoCs who sponsored them. Once at Lantana we had a boarder who used to call them 'little spies' gathering information for the Guardians."

"Really!"

"Well, she only lasted one term . . ." Both women laughed. The PoCs didn't tolerate any challenge to their Movement.

Mei-Lien continued, "Spies or not, who knows, but the thought of having an Assistant constantly in this house, privy to every movement, every conversation . . . and trust me, an Assistant would be *assigned*. I wouldn't get to choose. Just the thought . . . I don't want to lose the little privacy I have."

Mrs. Zhang decided to throw off the charade completely. "From what I've experienced, the PoC Movement is little more than religious pretension masking the moral tyranny of a devout and submissive majority. Oh, and financial tyranny! My God, the money they drain from the members! And who knows where it goes!" Mrs. Zhang could see a twinkle in Mei-Lien's eyes that encouraged her further. "It seems to me, the Founder puts more demands on the members than Jesus himself . . . and he's set up a system of control that dictators would admire. You realize I'm only part of the PoCs for your sake."

Mei-Lien smirked at her mother. "I came to that conclusion several years ago. I know you, Mom. There were plenty of times in the past when Scott would say or do something and I knew you would have liked to take a strip off him. But you'd sit there with this dull look in your eyes."

"Why didn't you say something?"

"I don't know, Mom . . . I wasn't sure of myself. I couldn't admit my doubts to myself, let alone to you . . . And Dad loved the Tans! He was always telling me what a great guy Scott was."

"Yes, he did love the Tans . . . But if he knew what was really going on . . ."

"I know, I know . . . It was so confusing."

"Mei-Lien," said Mrs. Zhang, "why do you put up with this? It's not the life you want!"

"Mom, how can I possibly leave?" Tears welled up and trickled down her cheeks. "I have five kids and now another almost here."

"I will help you."

"If I told Scott I wanted to leave, he'd be furious. The PoCs wouldn't stand for it. Mom, I'm so afraid I'd lose the kids. And you can be sure the Tans would come running to the defense of their golden boy. I've thought about it so many times. It's impossible."

CHAPTER 53

Andrew was abruptly pulled from his monthly departmental meeting and summoned to Mark Johnson's office, three stories up. By the time Andrew arrived, three other upper management officials had joined Mark and they quickly and gravely exchanged introductions.

"Some months back you expressed your concerns on the management and safety of the International Festival of Young Adults," said Mark. "Well, we've just received some alarming news regarding the event." Mark handed Andrew a newspaper article and he quickly read the story.

The Saturday overnight event and Sunday's concluding Mass were originally scheduled to take place in a vast meadow north of the host city. Two days ago an electrical storm had flashed a bolt of lightning that blew through the electrical wires of the imposing main stage and set it aflame. (The theme of this IFYA was "Kindle the Fire of Love" and the irony was not lost on the news reporter.)

The structural damage, requiring weeks of repair, precluded any possibility of restoring what remained. The massive altar, wired for an awe-inspiring light show during the evening musical extravaganza had, instead, flared into a fiasco. Critics, who had balked at the twelve million dollar tab for a venue that would be used for less than a day, were swift in their condemnation. But this did not deter the participants or their leaders. The IFYA director had stated, "Setbacks are only opportunities to let the power of God triumph. Satan will not be allowed to thwart this work of God."

With only days to prepare, the concluding ceremonies were being transferred to the site that would also host the opening event, an old military airport. A frantic effort was being made to fence off additional sections of land in view of the much larger crowd anticipated for the final events. Transport trucks were rushing back and forth from the defunct site to load barriers, tents and port-a-potties in order to beef up the inadequacies of the impromptu location.

Andrew set down the paper and leaned back in his chair. Mark continued, "Secure Star is offering travel insurance to US participants for this event. IFYA organizers around the country have been encouraging all participants to buy in and the response has been considerable. Before signing the contract, we carefully reviewed the reports of past IFYAs and analyzed the safeguards we were assured would be in place. But with this recent happening, we," Mark indicated the upper management present, "are concerned that the safety standards are not as high as we had been led to believe."

The four men looked at Andrew as Mark continued, "We want you to go as an observer and prepare a report."

"Why me?"

"Because, Andrew, you have the advantage of prior experience."

Andrew paused to consider the assignment.

"It's only a four to six hour flight, similar time zones. A friend of mine has a townhouse there that he's willing to lease. You can stay for a few days afterward and do some sightseeing. It begins in two days. I need an answer today. "

Andrew tapped his fingers on the arm of his chair. "If I go, I want to bring a couple of people: my wife, Rebecca, and an old friend who's also had experience with the IFYA."

"Three people?"

"You have no idea how massive and chaotic this event is."

Mark looked around at the others who nodded in agreement. "Okay. Get back to me in an hour."

Three days later, Andrew, Rebecca and Micah touched down in the host city with the IFYA in full swing. As soon as they landed, Andrew pulled out his phone and texted a message.

CHAPTER 54

Mrs. Zhang's cellphone chimed an incoming text. "I wonder who that could be."

"I'm surprised you heard it over the din," said Mei-Lien. She was playing music and folding the laundry with her mom on the couch while the children scurried about with their toys.

Mrs. Zhang went to the kitchen area and picked up her phone from the counter.

"Who is it?" asked Mei-Lien as she watched her mom scrutinize the text and type back a reply.

"It's Andrew."

"Andrew!" said Mei-Lien so loudly that her children paused and looked up.

Mrs. Zhang returned to the pile of clothes and she and Mei-Lien continued to fold until the kids were again engrossed in their play. Mrs. Zhang turned up the music.

"At some point . . . I wrote to Andrew and apologized for the way I treated him . . . and you. And I've sent him a Christmas card every year after that."

"How did you know where he lived?"

"I sent them through Fr. Hachette."

"Hachette . . . Fr. Hachette. It's been so long. He helped you?"

"He's become a dear friend."

171

A few moments passed.

"Did you ever hear back from Andrew?"

"After a few years. He began to send me a Christmas card in return. And then several years ago we started to email—or text . . . just a few times a year. I've let him know about your children. He tells me about his family, where he works. He knows what I think of the PoCs. Occasionally, he'll send me an article about the Movement he finds concerning. He's married now . . . to a woman named Rebecca."

Mei-Lien and her mother exchanged glances.

"Do you hate me for what I did? I often wonder how different . . ."

"I've wondered, too," said Mei-Lien wistfully. "But who knows . . . Would I have succumbed to the PoCs eventually and dropped Andrew on my own? He warned me about them, you know . . . And in the end, I doubted him . . . I doubted myself and chose the PoCs."

"And had you and Andrew gotten serious, I would have opposed you all the way. You know his brother is gay?"

Mei-Lien looked up, "Yes, he told me. I met him, Raph . . . at a breakfast."

"Right. That's when the FonS girl . . . what is her name . . .

"Casie?"

"Yes, Casie. She saw you with Andrew's family. She was also the one who followed you into the library. Oh, Mei-Lien, if I could go back . . ." Mrs. Zhang folded a few tops then continued, "Raph and his partner are raising a couple of kids—adopted them: twins with Down syndrome. Andrew's mother considers them grandchildren. Imagine how I would have reacted to that!"

Mei-Lien stared at her mother.

"What?" said Mrs. Zhang, seeing Mei-Lien's expression. "They've loved each other well over a decade and are raising two kids."

"You've changed . . . so much." Mei-Lien leaned over a pile of folded clothes and embraced her mother.

"Only because my eyes were opened by what happened to you. I'm so sorry I set you up at the Lantana."

The children looked over. Yelling, "Group hug, group hug!" they playfully joined their mother and grandmother, knocking down piles of folded clothes.

"I think it's time for a snack," said Mrs. Zhang, heading for her suitcase. As the kids were eating their treats, Mei-Lien restacked the clothes and went to the fridge for some cool water. "So what did the text say?"

"Andrew's just arrived at the IFYA. He's there for business."

CHAPTER 55

"I can't go without my sister. My mother said I CAN'T go without my sister."

Amy was still tired from the previous night's escapade: a three-hour musical rally and a long walk back to their assigned lodgings. The accommodations provided for their group, an outdoor assembly hall, was hardly accommodating. It was nothing more than a huge, covered, concrete slab. Sleeping outdoors offered some relief from the heat and humidity but the cracked, unyielding floor kept the guests tossing and turning throughout the night. To ward off the mosquitoes they either had to remain covered and deal with the heat, or slather themselves with repellent and try to ignore the incessant drone of the circling pests.

Early that morning, with Amy asleep beside her, Emily had been awakened by Nina, their Guardian. Excitedly she told her that a select group of young leaders from Hong Kong, Macau, Taiwan and Singapore were invited for breakfast with the Founder at the city centre. What a privilege! Amy needed her rest, she was told. Let her sleep. Emily was assured she would be back well before she and Amy were slated to be driven to a PoC centre for the night and the rest of the group began their hike to the site of the final festivities.

At the breakfast, the Founder spoke to the young people of the spiritual darkness shrouding Mainland China. Vehemently, he emphasized the urgency of bringing the light of Christ to the unbelievers of that vast nation. He told them he was counting on their self-sacrifice and leadership to venture forth: they were the future army of evangelizers he envisioned entering Chinese cities and towns with the Word of God!

But the Founder had arrived late and his zealous oration drifted and roved for more than an hour. Caught in snarled traffic, the driver of the elite Chinese evangelizers called Nina. There was no way Emily would make it back to the assembly hall before it was vacated by the group. Nina called Scott. They decided that Amy would go with her group to the festival site and Emily would join another PoC contingent. If the two groups happened to land up in nearby sections, Emily and Amy could possibly meet up at the site. If not, patience. These things happen. It was God's will.

At the news, Amy began to cry.

"Why do you allow yourself to become so upset!" chided Nina. "We are your family. These are your brothers and sisters." She pointed to the group gathering their belongings for the hike. "We're all going together. And you'll most likely meet Emily at the site. Offer it up!"

CHAPTER 56

The sun blazed relentlessly on the hundreds of thousands of young people making their way toward the festival site. Traffic had been blocked from the two-lane route leaving it free for the participants. Black asphalt, blistering in the heat, burned through the soles of sandals and shoes. Many young people trudged slowly, fatigued from days of heat, overcrowding, erratic meals, interminable lines and lack of sleep. When they could, intrepid hikers tromped past in the ditches. It was six hours before the massive group began to approach the defunct airport and was splintered off to the entrances of assigned sections.

~

Amy had lost awareness of everything but the heat. If anyone in their group remarked on the distance, the weight of their backpack, or their hunger and thirst, one member or other would begin a song and wave their banner, encouraging the others to offer up their sacrifices for the conversion of unbelievers. "We're almost there!" one of the Guardians would exclaim. Amy neither complained nor sang. She set one foot in front of the other, jostled forward by the PoC youth who surrounded her.

After seven hours and with empty water bottles, Amy's PoC group approached their entrance with a general sense of relief. It was short-lived. They soon came to a halt behind an enormous line, more like a human funnel, waiting to go through security. At this point, what patience remained, wore thin. Thirsty, hot, hungry and tired, the participants shoved and elbowed in order to maintain their place. The heat was insufferable. Several people nearby fainted and those assisting them shouted and pushed as they carried the unconscious participant to the front of the line for medical attention. The PoCs, depleted beyond a song or slogan, joined in the bedlam. With both hands, Amy grabbed onto the backpack in front of her and was literally dragged along by the crowd. Security guards gave fleeting glances to registration passes as the participants were spewed through the gates by the press of the crowd behind.

Once inside the grounds, Amy revived the hope of finding her older sister. For an hour their group slogged around fence-lined grids that hedged in multitudes of participants busy settling in. When at last they found their section, Amy anxiously scanned the crowd as they searched for some space to set up camp. There were no PoCs waiting for them. Some of their group cajoled and begged earlier arrivals for a spot to settle and Nina spread out a tarp. While others lay out their mats or left for the toilets, Amy curled up on one of the corners, spent and despondent.

CHAPTER 57

Andrew honked the horn of the quad and the crowd walking ahead turned and parted like the Red Sea.

"I feel guilty passing these kids," said Rebecca as the quad skirted along the sweat-plastered youth.

"Every time you feel guilty, take a picture," said Micah from the back seat. He was a freelance writer and, after this trip, he intended to write an exposé on the IFYA.

The three had registered for the IFYA concluding events and printed out their registration passes. To bolster their documentation, Andrew had made up official-esque IDs declaring them to be Authorized IFYA Secure Star Insurance Observers. He knew they would never get through the IFYA checkpoints in their rental car, so he had planned to rent a golf cart. Instead, when they pulled their car into the townhouse garage, they discovered the owner possessed a four-seater quad and immediately hijacked it for their purposes.

On the afternoon of the concluding events, Andrew, Rebecca and Micah made their way to the designated route. With their documentation, IFYA logos affixed to their quad, and the back of the quad stacked with bottled water, they passed through a checkpoint and merged with the walking participants. When the route became bogged down and the quad inched through, Micah handed out water.

Their goal was to take pictures that portrayed the organization of and participation in the final festivities as well as the conditions of the massive overnight site. While their pictures en route showed fervent youth united in faith, chanting prayers and slogans, they also revealed the flushed and bone-weary faces of less vocal participants. There were shots of inundated volunteers at water and food dispensing tents giving out the last of their supplies then abandoning the tents with thousands of participants still approaching.

In a particularly congested area Rebecca noticed a group of Asian youth waving a PoC banner and said to Andrew. "Didn't you say that two of Mei-Lien's daughters are here?"

In one of her periodic texts, Mrs. Zhang had informed Andrew that Mei-Lien was expecting another child and that she was going to Hong Kong to assist. She mentioned she was leaving earlier than expected as two of her granddaughters and their father were going to the IFYA. Andrew always shared with Rebecca the emails and texts he received from Mrs. Zhang. In fact, it was at Rebecca's urgings years before that he had increased his communication. Rebecca had marvelled at Mrs. Zhang when she heard not only of her apology but her continual attempts toward reconciliation, Christmas card after Christmas card—so different from her own mother.

In the rush of their preparations to depart for the IFYA, neither Andrew nor Rebecca had thought about Mrs. Zhang or her text sent a month or so before. But during the flight, as Andrew was about to doze off, Mrs. Zhang came to mind. He fired off a text to her as soon as he landed and told her of his concern about the site being used for the concluding festivities.

"Mei-Lien's daughters are *here*?" asked Micah, surprised.

"Micah, I forgot to tell you." Andrew filled in Micah about the first text. Then he continued, "Mrs. Zhang texted yesterday evening when you both were out getting supplies. The girls have come to the IFYA but are staying at a PoC centre for these final events."

"Thank God," said Rebecca. "This heat is horrendous."

As they drew near the site, Andrew circled around until they spotted the cargo entrance. A squad of jeeps and quads dropping off medical supplies and personnel were idling behind a truck waiting for clearance. Andrew pulled up with them and their quad managed to slip through.

CHAPTER 58

The sun was setting by the time a Guardian, one of Nina's colleagues, and several group members arrived with food packets and water. As they were passing out the rations, a muted roar from the front grew and spread through the field. The monitors flashed to life.

"We have a very special announcement! The Pope is with us tonight!" Participants leapt to their feet, cheering. What a surprise! The Pope had not been scheduled to come until the following day.

"Knowing the extraordinary effort to prepare this site for the festival and concluding Mass, the Pope chose to be with us tonight! He is arriving now for the prayer service to show his solidarity with all involved in this massive undertaking." More cheers. The emcee roused the crowd with a rhythmic clap and the chant, "Viva il Papa! Viva il Papa!"

~

Amy rolled over and began to rummage through her food pack. She knew she should eat but the thought made her nauseous. She sat up to take a sip from her bottled water. Her head spun. Nina motioned to her to draw closer and focus on prayer service being projected on the monitor. Amy gazed at her with a vacuous stare and then collapsed.

~

"I don't think you need to be transferred to the hospital tent," said the medic to Amy, Nina at her side. She lay Amy near the side of the tent, bent up her legs and put an ice pack on her forehead and one behind her neck. "I want to cool you down and get you rehydrated."

"When can she come back to the group?" asked Nina apprehensively. "I have over twenty other pilgrims that I am responsible for. I can't remain here long."

"I need to observe Amy for a couple of hours. Her blood pressure is low and I want to make sure she is rehydrated. Why don't you come back in about an hour or so and check up on her?"

"Oh, that would work! I'm only a fifteen-minute walk away. And Amy will be fine here with you." Cellphone numbers were exchanged and then she left.

"You better keep a copy of these numbers as well," said the medic. She handed Amy a folded piece of paper and Amy tucked it away in her back pocket.

"So what have you eaten today?" asked the medic.

"Breakfast and some snacks. The tent with the lunches ran out before we got there. And then we ran out of water."

The medic rose, shaking her head. "The stupidity..." she muttered to her companion who was taking the blood pressure of another dehydration victim.

"I warned you," she whispered back. "And it will only get worse."

The medic walked to the back of the tent and returned with a large bottle. "I want you to keep sipping this drink. It will help you get rehydrated. I'll be checking on you, but if you need anything, just call me."

A few minutes later the medic glanced over at Amy. The petite youth appeared younger than the fourteen years she claimed to be. Her lethargy and constricted answers, barely above a whisper, seemed to indicate something more than dehydration. The medic intended to keep an eye on her as long as she could until her shift ended the next morning.

CHAPTER 59

A ndrew parked the quad alongside a medical tent and the three stepped out. Micah and Andrew intended to investigate every aspect of the IFYA they had found disturbing during their previous experience to see if conditions had improved. From what they saw so far, there was no sign that the festival template had been refined or amended.

Rebecca talked to a nurse about the numbers of people coming for treatment and their ailments while Andrew and Micah took pictures as inconspicuously as possible. Already the medical tent was filled with young people, tubing curling from their arms to the IV bags hanging above. On they went, snapping pictures of the over-crowded sections, massive crowds at the port-a-potties, two-hour lines for food and water, insects hopping, flying or crawling about and, occasionally, even mice scurrying madly here and there. All was documented.

Rebecca was overpowered by the sheer immensity of the scene and the thousands upon thousands of participants who roamed about or were corralled in the array of fenced sections. When the Pope arrived, notwithstanding her previous experiences, she was still affected by the energy of the en masse clapping and chanting, "Viva il Papa! Viva il Papa!"

Andrew watched Rebecca astounded by the response of the crowd. He stood next to her and looked up at the monitor. "I don't believe it!" he exclaimed.

"What?" asked Rebecca. Andrew pointed to the monitor and waved to Micah to look as well.

On the monitor, standing directly behind the emcee and enthusiastically joining in with the chants and clapping was a group of clerics, one of whom Andrew recognized instantly. "It's the Reverend Theo Augustine O'Rourke warming up the crowd for the Pope!"

CHAPTER 60

By now it was completely dark. Occasional floodlights cast patches of light on the immense festival site. Nearby, a spotlight highlighted the medical tent.

"How are you doing?" said the medic as she approached Amy. "Still sipping?" Amy held up the bottle to show her progress. "Good."

After taking her vitals, the medic said, "I'm going to give your chaperone a call. You're blood pressure is coming up but it would be better if you stayed here for a couple more hours." Amy nodded.

As she dialled, Amy said, "Ask her if my sister is here."

"You have a sister here?"

"Emily. She came with a different group," she said, her voice quaking. "We were supposed to meet here."

The medic squatted near Amy and put the phone on speaker. She updated Nina who requested that Amy remain for the rest of the night—it would be difficult to transfer her back with the group in the dark. Then Amy asked about Emily.

"Yes, your sister is here," Amy brightened up and rose to her knees, "but in a completely different section—very close to the front. You see, your sacrifice brought a very big grace to Emily. You should rejoice for her." The medic rolled her eyes. Amy sat back down. "It is too hard for her to come to our section and, besides, you want her to be close to the Pope for the Mass tomorrow, no? You will see her tomorrow when we get back."

The medic put her cellphone in her pocket. Amy curled up against a tent pole. "Just the thought of walking back over that road tomorrow is making me sick."

"Don't worry about that for now. You'll feel better if you finish your drink and eat something. Then try to get some sleep." She walked to the back of the tent and made a call. Perhaps she could squeeze Amy on a bus.

CHAPTER 61

Most people were settled in, trying to get what sleep they could. Some trekked to and from the toilets. Others milled about determined to stay awake all night, too squeamish to lie amid the dirt, bugs, rodents and compacted humans. Drums and singing could be heard nearby and in the distance. Under the glow of intermittent floodlights, scattered groups of insomniacs danced.

A sudden gust of wind whirled through the site raising dust and debris. Some participants sat up, spitting out the grime. The gust abated, only to be followed by an even stronger gust and then another until there was no let up at all. Dirt, dried grass, plastic bottles and trash pummelled the crowd. Forked lightning lit the sky followed by a crack and immense thunder. Participants shifted from the tops of their tarps and mats and huddled underneath, protecting themselves from the windstorm and flying debris. Some people, finding it invigorating, laughed and danced about, oblivious to the tottering light poles and the service tents, straining against the wind.

~

"Do you think it will hold?" asked the medic to her companion as their tent swayed and bopped.

"Oh, God, I hope so."

They handed out space blankets to the people seated in the tent, helping them to wrap themselves against the wind. Just then a spotlight crashed over the top of the tent and rolled off to the side, ripping the tent and crashing to the ground. Someone screamed in pain.

The medic grabbed Amy and, with her companion, ushered the rest of the occupants out and down the roadway.

"You take them from here," said the medic. "Someone screamed. I'm going back."

~

The grass, withered by the heat, was ignited by the sparks from the shattered spotlight. The flames quickly spread and leapt through the gouge in the tent. A stack of empty cardboard boxes, depleted of medical supplies, was soon engulfed. The wind whipped the flames into a frenzy and quickly bore down on five portable oxygen tanks.

CHAPTER 62

People were screaming and running away from the fire as the medic pushed through toward the fallen light pole. A young man's leg was caught under the pole and several friends were trying to free him.

A blast and a soaring flame lit up the night.

"Bomb!" resounded throughout the section and hundreds more began to flee.

The medic and the friends of the trapped youth curled into a ball. Recouping, the medic yelled, "Get over here!" motioning the friends toward herself. Turning to the injured youth, she said, "This is going to hurt like hell." She then directed a couple to get ready to pull the youth from under his armpits; she and another grasped his waistband. The few remaining she sent toward the cracked end of the pole. "When I say go," she said, "you lift as much as you are able and we pull."

Another blast. Shrapnel flew from the tent, hitting the medic in the arm and one of the friends in the leg. They all dropped to the ground, those struck screeching in pain. But the medic quickly stood up and ordered them back to their positions. "Now!" she shouted. The young man howled but his leg released. They fled as quickly as they could, the injured supported by the others.

Three more blasts followed in quick succession and then a bellowing flame. "Suicide bomber!" was shouted by those fleeing. The fire spread beyond the tent, lashed about by the wind and feeding off the belongings left behind.

~

In the adjoining sections further away, trepidation increased as the blaze heightened and hundreds ran toward the exits urging those they passed to leave. Leaders, yelling through the wind and thunder, ordered their groups to walk calmly toward the exit. But when the three blasts erupted and the blaze shot up, pandemonium ensued.

CHAPTER 63

Nina, horrified, stared at the blaze coming from the area of the medical tent. Amy! Yet how could she leave the other youths who were stumbling blindly through their section, shielding their eyes from the grit blown up by the wind, being pushed this way and that by the throng? Decisively she turned away and focused on herding her group from the site.

The light poles swayed menacingly, throwing their beams erratically across the ground. A sting whipped Nina's cheek, then several more, her arm. A few moments later the clouds opened and pelted the crowd with driving rain. The screaming and shoving were relentless as friends tried to regroup and flee at the same time. And as the downpour mixed with the dust, participants slipped, skidded and collided in the mud. Although Nina tried to keep her group together, it was barely possible to see. A light pole behind them crashed to the ground, then all the lights went out.

∼

Fire trucks and emergency vehicles on site were hindered from approaching the blaze by the screaming hordes and the metal barriers that had been flipped over into the lanes. It was too perilous to drive through the abandoned sections not knowing if the sleeping bags, backpacks and tarps masked someone who had collapsed or been trampled unconscious. To make matters worse, there were downed floodlights with live wires whipping around in the rain and wind. The electricity was cut leaving the departing pilgrims in total darkness.

CHAPTER 64

The Pope, archbishop, executive director of the IFYA, and the Pope's personal secretary were seated comfortably in the spacious living room of the archbishop's residence sipping their midnight quaffs. They commented with elation on the success of the events during the past few days and the immensity and devotion of the crowds present for the evening prayer. The phone of the executive director vibrated but, considering it rude to interrupt this casual and exclusive conversation with the Pope, he ignored it.

~

Rev. Theo O'Rourke had been part of the Pope's entourage to and from the festival site but not invited to the intimate gathering in the living room. He and several other members of the IFYA organizing committee waited in a reception room near the front door laughing and exchanging anecdotes. Simultaneously their cellphones vibrated and rang with incoming alerts. As they scanned their news feeds a sense of dread permeated the room. The men looked at each other in disbelief. Theo rose abruptly and went to the living room. He cracked the door and motioned to the executive director.

"You better call out the archbishop."

Once the archbishop was in the hallway, the executive director asked Theo to hold up his phone. Newscasters on the festival site were reporting through their cellphones, citing their power source had been cut off. Conflicting reports from those fleeing the scene ranged from "tornado," to "fire," to "bombs." Participants stumbling forward on the road back to the city were randomly interviewed weeping, disoriented, separated from their groups, worried about their friends, unsure where to go since their lodgings at schools and church halls were locked.

"Oh, Christ, oh Christ!" said the archbishop as he leaned against the wall. "How? Why?"

The archbishop's phone vibrated. The communication director was on the line. "We need a statement — immediately. 'The archbishop is following the situation with grave concern. He urges faithful to open their homes to the participants.'"

"Yes, that fine," he said, still in shock. He ended the call without another word.

"We have to tell the Pope," said the archbishop.

Theo watched from the door as the archbishop and the executive director returned to the living room. The Pope's personal secretary was sitting near the pontiff, cellphone in hand. They stared at each other in stunned silence.

～

Theo walked back toward the reception room. The members of the organizing committee were in disarray, swiping through news feeds, talking on the phone, sitting on the edge of their chairs or pacing back and forth. Theo slipped out the front door unnoticed.

Back in his hotel room, Theo changed from his clericals to a polo shirt and slacks, stuffed his belongings into a suitcase, and caught a cab to the airport. He was merely an advisor to the IFYA organizing committee, he acquitted himself, nothing more.

CHAPTER 65

From the hospital tent, Andrew, Rebecca and Micah watched in horror as the flames shot up across the field. They had intended to leave the site and return the next day. But with nightfall, they decided the chances of them getting lost were greater than the amount of gas in the quad. So they had parked next to the hospital tent and chatted with the staff or observed the goings-on among the participants.

The windstorm had been alarming enough but when they heard the blast and saw the flames leap up, the three joined the medical staff, now in conference on how to prepare for whatever calamity was headed their way. The blinding rain, the stampeding participants and, now, the utter darkness brought a whole new level of trepidation. A nurse activated a battery-operated generator and some of the lights flickered back on in the tent. The lead staff tried to contact her immediate supervisor on site, but the line was busy. Other emergency contacts could only report that the cause of the blasts and fire were unknown and that the power had been cut due to live wires in the rain.

There was no evacuation plan or vehicles to transport the more than two hundred patients to the city. The staff determined that walking offsite in the darkness and driving rain was more risky than staying put, so they decided to hunker down until help could be provided. Andrew, Rebecca and Micah informed and calmed the patients while the staff organized the tent for the injured they knew would be arriving.

CHAPTER 66

It was late afternoon when Mei-Lien and Mrs. Zhang left the relative coolness of the park and walked home. When they entered the apartment, Mei-Lien pulled out her phone and noticed several missed messages. She had turned on "Do Not Disturb" during Mass and had forgotten to turn it off.

Check the news. Accident at the IFYA was a text from a PoC mother.

Mei-Lien flicked to a news feed and brought up the IFYA. Explosions, stampede, driving rain, missing people. She felt a flood of panic and then immense relief. Yes, she had been right to forbid Emily and Amy to attend the final events. "Pampering" and "coddling" had been levelled against her but she had not backed down: it was prudence. At the same time, she was distraught for the young people caught up in the disaster, many of whom she knew.

"What is it?" asked Mrs. Zhang, seeing her daughter blanch.

Mei-Lien signalled with her eyes. "Time for baths!" she said to her children. "Peter, you're first. Grace, would you run the water for him? John Paul, please take this bag of toys and put them where they belong."

With the children occupied, Mei-Lien showed the news feed to her mother.

"My God, this is terrible! Where are the girls?"

"They're at the PoC centre. I'm calling now." Before leaving on the trip, all the parents had been given a list of PoC contacts in the host city. A busy signal buzzed in Mei-Lien ear. Alarm shot through her veins. *The girls are fine. Of course they were,* she told herself. But she could not relax until she heard their voices. She tried the number several times with the same result. Nina's phone was unavailable. One by one she tried the numbers on the list.

Mrs. Zhang went into Mei-Lien's bedroom and phoned Andrew.

"What's going on?" she asked anxiously.

"Utter mayhem." He went on to describe the situation. "Thank God, Mei-Lien's kids didn't come to the site."

Mrs. Zhang glanced out of the office door. Mei-Lien was tapping out another number. "We still haven't been able to contact them . . . or anyone over there."

"Let me know when you do. And if there is anything I can do to help, let me know. Rebecca and Micah are also here. We're more than ready to give a hand. Anything at all, you understand?"

Mrs. Zhang swallowed hard. "Yes, Andrew. I'll be in touch."

~

John Paul watched as his grandmother moved his mother, phone in hand, from the couch to her bedroom and close the door.

"What's the matter?" he asked.

"Your mom wants to talk to your sisters but she is having a hard time making the connection. Why don't you come and help me with supper."

Every so often Mrs. Zhang poked her head in the bedroom. Each time Mei-Lien just shook her head.

"Mei-Lien, the kids have all bathed and eaten supper," said Mrs. Zhang after checking in and seeing the disappointment on Mei-Lien's face. "Come out and say good night. They're getting worried. As soon as they're down, you and I can continue calling."

~

Mei-Lien turned on a soothing music channel and settled her children. "Why are we going to bed so early?" asked Grace.

"Because we've had a big day outside and now it's time to relax. If you don't want to sleep right away, turn on your bedside light and read. And Peter, you can sleep in Grandma's bed!"

Back in the bedroom, Mei-Lien and her mom divided the list and attempted each phone number again. Finally, an answer at the PoC centre! Mei-Lien explained who she was and asked to speak with her daughters. "Daughters? Girls? One moment . . . There's so much going on here . . ." The phone passed to another who seemed more rattled than the previous. Mei-Lien insisted that her daughters were there and would they please bring them to the phone. At last, someone higher in command came on the line. No, the Tan sisters were not there but she could try another residence closer to the festival site. When Mei-Lien hung up her hands were shaking so badly that Mrs. Zhang took her phone, tapped in the number Mei-Lien had been given and put the phone on speaker mode.

"Let me check . . . hmm . . . yes, yes, Tan. Emily Tan is here," said the Guardian.

"And Amy? Is Amy with her?" asked Mei-Lien anxiously.

"Amy? Who is Amy?" asked the Guardian nervously. "We have so many kids pouring in here. It's hard to keep track—"

"Amy is my daughter! Put Emily on the line!"

"She's not near the—"

"I want to speak with my daughter. Put her on the phone—now!"

Several minutes later Emily came to the phone. As soon as she heard her mother's voice, she burst into tears. "Amy's not here. We don't know where she is."

Mei-Lien forced calmness into her voice. "Emily, Emily, take some deep breaths . . . We'll find her. Okay, now tell me what happened."

Emily told her mother about the events of the morning, the traffic jam and Nina's call to her father giving permission for the girls to attend the concluding ceremonies. Mei-Lien seethed within but retained her outward calm.

"Emily, this is very important. I need to know exactly where you are." She could hear Emily talking to someone nearby and was soon able to give the address. "I don't want you to go anywhere else without *my* permission. You stay put until you hear from me. You sit somewhere near this phone and don't move no matter what the Guardians say—you tell them to call me! Are we clear?"

"Yes," said Emily, her voice cracking.

"We will find Amy."

After assuring each other of their love, Mei-Lien hung up and exploded in a volley of sobs. Her fury with Scott and the PoCs had no words and her concern for Amy riddled her with anxiety. Mrs. Zhang took her in her arms and swayed.

"Mei-Lien, Mei-Lien, calm down or you'll be giving birth on top of everything else." Gradually, she had Mei-Lien breathing deeply and drinking water. Together they stood up and walked to the kitchen sink. Mei-Lien splashed her face with water and drew the lingering drops through her hair. She turned decisively to her mother.

"I'm done, Mom. I am so done with this."

CHAPTER 67

The rain had stopped. Andrew, Rebecca and Micah gathered near the entrance of the medical tent. The coming dawn cast an ominous aura across the abandoned festival site. Contours of deserted encampments seemed to rise from the earth like spectres foreshadowing an ongoing nightmare.

Andrew's phone rang. "Mrs. Zhang, how are you doing?"

"We need your help."

~

Micah assisted the patients as they boarded the first of the buses sent to evacuate the site and then he hopped on board as well. Andrew and Rebecca climbed in the quad and sped off to comb the festival site for Amy. They hadn't gone far before they were stopped by the military. No unauthorized persons were allowed on the site, they were informed. And no amount of insistence, pleading or remonstration would persuade the soldiers otherwise. Search teams were scouring the site as they spoke. If Amy is here, those authorized would find her and inform the authorities—all the participants were wearing their registration passes. To make sure their instructions were followed, the soldiers escorted the quad off the site.

~

The sun climbed higher in the sky, broiling Andrew and Rebecca as they inched along the designated route. The road was still blocked to routine traffic; however, emergency vehicles whipped past them continually. Whenever Andrew and Rebecca could not see clearly into the ditches and the fields beyond, they would stop the quad and walk amid the shrubs and stands of tall grass.

Both Andrew and Rebecca knew that Amy could be anywhere: back at the site, along the route or taken in by another group. Given the chaotic, uncoordinated communication they had witnessed so far, it would be hours before youth separated from their groups were located. Still Andrew and Rebecca carried on.

Two hours passed. Andrew was about to call Mrs. Zhang with his third unproductive report when Rebecca noticed a sliver of colour within a copse of shrubs. Andrew slammed on the brakes and both flew out of the quad, scrabbled down and up the side of the ditch, and ran over to the shrubs. Lying amid the sprigs was a young Asian girl.

~

Rebecca sat in the back seat of the quad, Amy in her lap. Andrew wrapped her with a space blanket they had been given at the hospital tent and curled her legs into the neighbouring seat.

"Amy, Amy, can you hear me?" Rebecca asked softly as she gently rocked Amy back and forth. Amy nodded slightly. Andrew watched in admiration as Rebecca engaged and soothed the traumatized girl—a trait that had initially awakened his interest in Rebecca.

"I'm Rebecca and this is Andrew." Andrew drew near so Amy could see him. "We're both friends of your mother." Amy quivered. "Would you like to speak to your mother?" Tears welled in Amy's eyes and rolled down her cheeks. "We're going to call her right now. But before we do, I need you to drink something." While she took a few sips from a water bottle, Andrew called Mrs. Zhang.

"We found her.

CHAPTER 68

Mrs. Zhang rifled through her suitcase and tossed out almost everything. They had to finish before dawn, before the children woke up.

"Are you almost finished?"

"Done," said Mei-Lien as she hit the send button and closed her laptop.

"Good. You need to start packing," said Mrs. Zhang as she laid her suitcase in a corner of Mei-Lien's room. "Focus on what means the most to you. Stuff can be replaced. One bag only."

Mrs. Zhang had managed to change her ticket and secure airline seats for Mei-Lien and the children: non-stop. "You said you had the passports. Where are they?"

Mei-Lien went to the closet and moved a couple of plastic storage containers revealing a small safe.

"They're locked in that safe?" said Mrs. Zhang, incredulous. "Any thief could carry it away."

"It's fire-proof."

"Mei-Lien if this apartment building went up in flames that little locked box would do nothing for you."

"Scott is adamant about these things. I have the key right here."

From a top shelf in a far back corner, Mei-Lien pulled out a small metal box, opened the latch, and stared inside. "It's not here."

"The bastard took it with him."

Mei-Lien sat on a chair, staring in disbelief at the box. Scott had purchased the safe shortly after they arrived. He had kept one key and given Mei-Lien the other. *Put it in a safe spot,* he'd said. *In case of an emergency, we'll both have a key.* Then he proceeded to secure all their essential documents in the safe. It had never occurred to Mei-Lien to hide the location of her key from her husband nor had she ever needed to access the safe. Scott was always there to open it when necessary.

The upheaval of the last several hours had left Mei-Lien emotionally drained but this further proof of control and deception removed any regrets regarding her decision to leave. Indignation filled her veins and solidified her resolve.

"If he thinks that pathetic hunk of iron is going to deter me!" Mei-Lien got up, went to the storage closet and pulled out a beleaguered cardboard box. Mrs. Zhang took the box from Mei-Lien and brought it to the kitchen counter. The box contained a mishmash of tools, nuts and bolts, fasteners and hooks but its most prized occupant was an electric drill.

~

"Three! That's all?" said Mei-Lien as she opened the pouch that held the bits.

"Just go slow and steady," said Mrs. Zhang.

Mei-Lien and her mother laid the safe on a mat in the bedroom and Mei-Lien positioned the drill. After a few minutes of boring, Mrs. Zhang said, "Maybe a little more pressure than that."

The bit broke immediately. "Shit," said Mrs. Zhang.

Mei-Lien didn't even look at her mother as she replaced the bit, sweat dripping off her forehead.

"I won't say another word," said Mrs. Zhang as she sat on a chair and rested her face in her hands.

Ten minutes later, Mei-Lien broke through. Mrs. Zhang jumped up and crouched near her daughter. Using a screwdriver, Mei-Lien turned the latch. She took a deep breath, opened the lid, and began to flip through the hanging files. Baptismal certificates, first communion, confirmation ... marriage licence ... academic records. With increasing apprehension, Mei-Lien went through them again. No passports.

"Shit, shit, shit!" said Mrs. Zhang, standing and throwing up her arms in frustration.

Mei-Lien lifted out the files and threw them on the floor. She slumped against the wall, tears streaming down her face.

Mrs. Zhang turned around and looked down at her daughter but her gaze shifted to the open safe. "What's that?"

Mei-Lien wiped her eyes and leaned over the safe. Lying flat across the bottom was a piece of stiff black card stock at odds with the black enamelled sides of the safe. "What the hell?" She plucked at the corner of the sheet and gently lifted up. It was the front cover of a black file folder. Lying side by side within were four passports.

CHAPTER 69

"I hope you like what I picked out," said Micah.

As Andrew drove the quad, Rebecca had called Micah with the news that Amy had been found. "She needs an outfit. Find something, anything!"

There was a small boutique and gift shop in the townhouse/condo complex and Micah had chosen a few items he hoped would fit.

Rebecca gave a quick glance to the clothes on the bed and nodded her approval. Her main concern was reviving Amy with a warm bath and some nourishment. Under normal circumstances, she would have brought Amy to a doctor for a thorough check-up, but their situation was anything but normal and there did not appear to be any serious injury. And from what she had seen at the medical tent, the health facilities would be deluged.

Amy settled into the sudsy water. Rebecca gently supported her neck and poured water over her hair, once, twice, over and over; lathering and rinsing while Amy's sore, bruised and mosquito-bitten body soaked. As Rebecca finished rinsing her hair, Amy turned and looked directly at her.

"Do you love my mother?" she asked softly.

"I do. She's a very brave woman. And I know she loves you very much."

"I love her, too."

"Soon you'll be with her again. We're going to pick up Emily and then we're flying off to be with your mother."

Tears filled her eyes. "Thank you," she whispered.

~

While Rebecca was occupied with Amy, Andrew and Micah hovered over Andrew's laptop and his tiny, thermal printer.

"Print out a few copies," said Micah. "I don't want to take any chances."

When the last of the sheets slid out, Micah folded and tucked the documents into his shoulder bag.

"You have everything you need? Passport? Phone charged?" asked Andrew.

"Yes, Mom," said Micah, and looking out the window, "Here's the taxi."

"Remember, you pay whatever it takes to hold that taxi."

Micah saluted and left.

~

Amy emerged from the bedroom supported by Rebecca. The transformation from the mud-smeared, ratty-haired youth was astounding. Though still listless, Amy's eyes met Andrew's and she smiled slightly. Her hair was pulled back, outlining the delicate features of her face, and the long sundress covered many of her bruises.

"You're looking much better, Amy," said Andrew. "How do you feel?"

"Better."

Rebecca gave Amy a slight squeeze. "I want you to try and have a little something to eat and then we'll be on our way."

Micah had prepared some sandwiches and fruit but, instead, Rebecca offered Amy some crackers and the rehydrating drink she'd picked up at the medical tent. "Just sips and tiny bites. I'm going to change my clothes. I'll be back in a few minutes."

Andrew had freshened up after Micah left so when Rebecca came out of the bedroom, Andrew grabbed her carry-on luggage. While he loaded it in the rental car Rebecca assisted Amy into the back seat.

CHAPTER 70

"Scott is certainly keeping a low profile," said Mrs. Zhang as she gathered up all the belongings she had removed from her suitcase and moved them behind some boxes in the storage closet.

The last time Mei-Lien had heard from Scott was early Sunday morning before the church services and their picnic at the park. She was sure he was well aware of the tragedy at the IFYA.

"He probably thinks I'm in the dark about Amy. I imagine he's holding out, waiting for Nina to give him a call to say everyone is accounted for . . . And we know that hasn't happened."

The PoC families involved in the IFYA were aware that Mei-Lien had forbidden Emily and Amy to go to the concluding events and considered her fortunate—her daughters were safe. Their focus was on their own children, anxiously waiting to hear they were located and unharmed. One mother called Mei-Lien and lamented that she had not set up the same restriction for her son and daughter.

Mei-Lien felt deeply for this mother but maintained her ruse. No one must know that Amy had been found until the last possible moment.

CHAPTER 71

"Micah, are you ready?" Andrew stood on the sidewalk holding his cellphone to his ear.

"Yes, right out in front."

"Okay, hold on." Andrew tapped in another number. "I'm on my way in. Are we all connected?"

"We're with you," said the voices from the phone.

Andrew walked up the broad, stone steps to the main entrance of the regional PoC centre and rang the bell. Decorative concrete bricks framed in the door and windows adding elegance to the pale salmon stucco that covered the rest of the formidable building. After several moments, he heard a latch slide and the door opened.

"I'm from Secure Star Insurance. I need to speak with Nina Bover."

"Umm . . ." said the woman, furrowing her brow, "I'm not sure if that will be possible."

"Well, make it possible. If I don't speak with her in five minutes, I'm calling the police," said Andrew sternly.

"Just one moment." The woman went to close the door but Andrew had anticipated the move and stepped into the entrance.

"Stay here," said the woman, glowering at Andrew. "I'll find someone to speak with you."

The relative calm outside the door was in stark contrast to the commotion within. On the other side of the spacious, marble-floored entrance were wide French doors that opened to a courtyard. Ordinarily, Andrew imagined, it would be a serene, private garden, sheltered from the hustle and bustle of the world outside. Today it was replete with young people, tattered and muddy. They lay on the ground; sat cross-legged leaning forward, faces in their hands; or were curled against the inside walls and pillars. A number of adults flitted among them, clipboards in hand, appearing to gather names and information. Some adults passed out bottled water while others assisted youths who hobbled through the throng toward an opened interior door at the rear of the courtyard.

A side door opened and Andrew swung around to a tall woman in a crisp, white blouse, long, brown skirt and sandals. She looked like she just stepped out of the shower, her damp hair pulled back in a loose bun. She regarded Andrew closely, her demeanour both haggard and vexed.

"You wanted to speak with me?" she said curtly.

"If you are Nina Bover."

"I am," she said as she crossed her arms.

"I'm here from Secure Star Insurance representing Mei-Lien Tan." Andrew saw Nina grip her arms a little more tightly. "I understand her daughter, Amy, has been missing since the stampede at the festival site early this morning. Is this true?"

"A number of young people were separated from their groups." Nina countered brusquely. "An effort—"

"Is it true that Amy Tan is missing?" said Andrew, adamant.

"She has not yet returned, no."

"I'm here to inform you that you are hereby relieved of your duties with regard to both Emily and Amy." Andrew passed Nina a document signed by Mei-Lien. "You went against Mrs. Tan's explicit instructions that neither Emily nor Amy were to be separated or participate in the concluding events at the festival site. I'm here to pick up their passports, find Amy and bring both Emily and Amy to their mother."

Nina glanced at the document. "It's impossible."

Andrew lifted up the phone he had been carrying. "Mrs. Tan, are you still connected? I'm putting the phone on speaker."

"Nina, give the passports to Mr. Covick, now," said Mei-Lien firmly.

Nina rubbed her forehead with one hand and dropped the other arm to her side.

"Nina!"

"Yes, I hear you," said Nina impatiently.

"If you do not, I will contact the American Embassy and inform them that you are holding my daughters against my will."

Nina turned and went back through the side door.

"Micah?" said Andrew into the phone.

"I heard everything. I'm already at the door."

"And the taxi?"

"The driver is getting wealthier by the minute."

CHAPTER 72

Nina climbed the stairs and walked down the open hallway that overlooked the courtyard. She paused to gaze at the hundreds of youths crammed below. Her stomach lurched. She arrived at the PoC centre with only four of the twenty participants under her care. Several more had since called in from other locations. But not Amy. Where was Amy? And now this Mr.—Nina looked at the document—Andrew Covick. Hired by Mei-Lien! My, God. So Mei-Lien knew.

Nina had call Scott as soon as she could after returning to the PoC centre. He'd been trying to contact her for hours but her phone died from using it as a flashlight on the road home. He would make some calls, he assured her. Amy would be found. And he, and only he, would take care of informing Mei-Lien, maybe waiting until he could travel back to Hong Kong. In her condition, he told Nina, it would be better if she heard the news from him in person.

Nina pushed away from the bannister and headed to her room. She hadn't slept at the outdoor assembly hall with the young participants. A group of PoC volunteers watched over the sleeping participants, relieving Nina. She was driven to the PoC centre each night and returned in the morning. In her room, Nina opened a bureau drawer and pulled out the bundle of passports. She should call Scott.

At any other time she would not have hesitated. She had little regard for Scott's chunky, lackluster wife and flouted her empty threat.

Nina knew if Scott forbid her to hand over the passports—and he would—then Mei-Lien's request would be nil and void. Today, however, replaying over and over in her mind was the sight of the blast coming from the area of the medical tent. Rumours were circulating that some participants were dead. Two-thirds of her youth were still at large. She hadn't slept in over twenty-four hours. Nina's throat constricted and she paced to calm her throbbing heart. She was tired of placating the Founder's prize bull. Nina flipped through the passports and pulled out the Tan sisters'.

~

"Guard these with your life," said Andrew as he handed the passports to Rebecca, moved in behind the steering wheel and drove off. Once they were several blocks away from the PoC centre, Andrew pulled over and called Micah. "Where are you?"

CHAPTER 73

A dishevelled youth opened the door of the PoC hostel. Micah waved a folded sheet of paper declaring loudly and urgently, "I have an important document for Emily Tan," and squeezed in. As soon as he entered, the chaos was evident. Young people squatted, sat, or lay in every available space, right up to the main entrance. Micah did not wait for assistance. He walked through the open hallway doors, repeating his cry, "Emily Tan, Emily Tan. An important document for Emily Tan." An Asian girl toward the middle of the hallway stood and made her way over the tangle of legs and arms.

Micah looked up and down the hallway. Where were the staff? Obviously, they were too overrun to be monitoring the corridors.

"Are you Emily Tan?" Micah asked the girl who approached him.

"Yes," and, as if on cue, she held up her registration pass still dangling from a lanyard around her neck.

Micah held up his folded document, "I have a message from your mother, Mei-Lien Tan. I'll explain everything as soon as we are out of the building."

At the sound of her mother's name, Emily teared up and followed Micah to the main entrance. As he opened the door, a large, young man, rumpled and dirty as the rest, hollered from the hallway door, "Just where do you think you're going?"

Micah took Emily by the shoulder and pushed her out the door. He passed the document to a nearby youth and said, "Give this to him," indicating the young man who had jumped into command. Then Micah, too, walked out the door.

"Emily, I have your mom on the phone. You have to walk with me as quickly as you can." He gave Emily his phone and put his arm behind her back, guiding her down the street to the waiting taxi.

"Emily, go with Micah," said Mei-Lien. "He's a friend of mine. He is taking you to Amy."

~

As the taxi driver approached the airport, he pulled over at a location Micah had requested earlier. The driver smiled broadly and waved as Micah and Emily exited the taxi. He had made a week's wage in one run.

During all this time, Emily talked with her mother. Micah hadn't understood a word: they spoke together in Mandarin.

"I know you are tired, but can you walk a bit further?" Micah asked Emily. Emily nodded and continued talking to her mother, occasionally wiping away her tears. A few blocks later, his phone began to chime. Taking it from Emily, Micah said to Mei-Lien, "Andrew's back on the line. We'll call you soon."

"Andrew, we're near the airport," said Micah. "Yeah, at a place I felt least likely to bump into any IFYA participants—in front of the Metro Casino!"

CHAPTER 74

"Go take a shower," Mrs. Zhang told her daughter. "The kids will be up soon. I'll go after you."

Mother and daughter had cleaned up the bedroom, leaving the closet as it appeared before. The passports were now in Mei-Lien's shoulder bag next to her laptop and all the other documents. The only items she had put in her mother's suitcase were a few photo albums which she covered with a knitted scarf and hat.

"You brought winter clothes to Hong Kong?" Mrs. Zhang asked. Mei-Lien just shrugged.

"Is there anything else that is important to you? Think!"

"I just want my children."

~

"Why are we getting up so early?" asked John Paul as he and his sisters shuffled out of their bedroom.

"Because we don't want the sun to be lonely," teased Mei-Lien. "Look! It's already up, just waiting for us."

"Today let's have some fun," said Mrs. Zhang. "Why don't all of you put on your favourite clothes?"

While Mrs. Zhang helped her grandchildren choose their clothes, Mei-Lien prepared their breakfast. Once they had eaten, Mrs. Zhang proposed another game.

"If you were going on a long, long trip, what would be your favourite things to bring? What toys and books?" Their personal space was so limited that it didn't take long for the children to return with their chosen items. "Next challenge: are you able to fit all this into your backpacks?" The children competed with each other and Mrs. Zhang helped them to maximize space.

While Mrs. Zhang kept the children occupied, Mei-Lien made a sweep of her eldest daughters' shelves and drawers and packed what she could in the suitcase. Back in the main room the children proudly showed her their backpacks of treasures. Scattered around were some toys and books that couldn't fit and had to be left aside. Mei-Lien casually picked these up and brought them back to their room.

When she returned, Mei-Lien sat next to her mother on the couch. The children were gathered around getting Grandma's treats for prizes. But before they opened their packages Mei-Lien said, "Grandma is going to be leaving us today."

"Isn't she going to stay until Daddy comes home?" Grace asked.

"Emily and Amy will be with us soon. But I have a surprise. We're going to the airport with Grandma and you can eat your treats on the way. Bring your backpacks so if we have to wait for her flight, you'll have something to keep you busy."

"And we're all ready, so we are leaving right now," said Mrs. Zhang.

Mei-Lien took one last walk around the apartment as John Paul help his grandmother roll her suitcase into the hallway and the younger children ran for the elevator. Mrs. Zhang escorted the children down to the curb in front of their apartment complex and hailed a taxi. As the driver loaded her suitcase and the backpacks in the trunk, the children climbed in the back seat. Anxious to be leaving, Mrs. Zhang turned toward the apartment building and waved at Mei-Lien to hurry.

"I'm coming, I'm coming," said Mei-Lien as the main door slammed behind her. Mother and daughter were both about to enter the taxi when down the street a voice shouted, "Mei-Lien, Mei-Lien!" It was a Guardian.

CHAPTER 75

"Shit, shit, shit," breathed Mrs. Zhang.

The Guardian was panting when she reached the taxi. "I was just coming to visit, Mei-Lien. Where are you going?" she asked with concern.

"Oh, my mother is leaving . . ."

"Leaving?" Then directing her question to Mrs. Zhang, she said, "I thought you were going to stay until Scott returned?"

"Something came up," said Mei-Lien. "Patience. These things happen. It's God's will."

Mrs. Zhang stared at Mei-Lien, silently entreating her to go easy with the rhetoric.

"I could stay with you until Scott is back. It would be no trouble at all."

"No, no, that won't be necessary. Soon I'll have my girls with me. I'll be fine. Besides, Scott is a man of faith. He knows that God always takes care."

"But where are *you* going?" the Guardian persisted. Bending down, she peered at the children in the back seat, "And all the children, too?"

"I'm accompanying my mother to the airport."

"Do you think that's necessary? I mean, in your condition? I'm sure your mother can manage by herself. There are so many porters available to help at the airport."

"I would like to spend this time with my daughter," responded Mrs. Zhang, barely able to mask her irritation.

"But not with the children, certainly. I can watch them. It will be so much easier for you."

"I want to go with Grandma," piped up Peter.

"Me, too," exclaimed Grace and John Paul.

"We're going as a family," said Mei-Lien firmly.

The taxi driver honked his horn and the resolve in Mei-Lien's voice stopped any further insistence.

"We'll see you at the encounter this evening then," said the Guardian.

"Maybe not. It depends on when we get back."

Mei-Lien climbed in the back seat while Mrs. Zhang slid in the front. When the cab pulled away, Mrs. Zhang let out a stream of Chinese expletives.

"What did Grandma say?" asked John Paul.

The taxi driver laughed and Mei-Lien groaned.

CHAPTER 76

Andrew slowed as he approached the casino.

"There they are," exclaimed Rebecca, pointing.

As soon as the car came to a stop, Emily opened the door, jumped inside and cradled her sister. Andrew, Rebecca and Micah watched as the two silently held each other, crying softly. As Andrew drove, Rebecca texted Mrs. Zhang and Mei-Lien that the girls were reunited and they were all headed to the airport.

The exit into the main terminal was clogged with traffic but Andrew bypassed it all, taking a route marked for air cargo depots.

"Are you planning on loading us in a crate?" asked Rebecca.

"That's why I packed up the food at the condo," smiled Andrew.

Micah was guiding Andrew from the GPS on his phone but even he looked baffled.

Andrew had kept Mark Johnson abreast of the disaster at the festival site. Given the chaos, Andrew told his boss, the airlines would most likely be in a jumble. Could he arrange alternate transportation home should that be necessary? Mark provided Andrew with a contact.

"We're headed to an FOB—fixed-base operator—a terminal for private jets," said Andrew. "Sometimes it pays to work for a national insurance company."

CHAPTER 77

Mei-Lien padded down the narrow aisle of the plane holding Peter's hand while Mrs. Zhang herded the other two children from behind. They found their seats in the middle of the midsection. Mei-Lien slid in, protecting her extended belly, followed by the three children and capped by Mrs. Zhang. Mei-Lien hadn't slept for over a day; yet during the three hours they waited for their flight she could not bring herself to close her eyes for fear of being accosted by a Guardian, or a PoC member, unlikely as that might be.

About an hour before boarding, Mrs. Zhang asked the children if they would like to come on an adventure and see where Grandma lived. At first they were bewildered. Mei-Lien assured them that their two sisters would meet them there and that Daddy was sure to follow. They excitedly joined in on the plan.

At last the doors were secured and the plane began to taxi down the runway. As the engines gunned and the plane lifted, Mei-Lien allowed her exhaustion to overwhelm her. Before they had gained their altitude, her head was already leaning to the side, her mouth drooped open in sleep.

CHAPTER 78

The mid-morning sun shone through the skylights at the international terminal. The flight from Hong Kong had arrived an hour before. At any moment, Andrew expected Mrs. Zhang, Mei-Lien and her children to come through the opaque doors of the airport customs.

~

Andrew, Rebecca, Micah, Emily and Amy had arrived the night before and stayed at a nearby hotel. This morning they dropped Andrew off at the terminal and now waited in a nearby cellphone waiting lot, ready to pull up in the arrivals zone as soon as they heard Mei-Lien and her family had passed through customs. Andrew had rented a passenger van to usher all of them to Mrs. Zhang's home, about an hour away. Though the sisters were anxious to be reunited with their family, Amy was still very weak and Emily was exhausted. So Andrew and Rebecca decided it was best for them to wait in the van.

~

The door opened. Instantly, Andrew recognized Mrs. Zhang and Mei-Lien.

"They're here!" he shouted into his phone.

Andrew had no idea what to expect from Mei-Lien . . . or himself. It had been almost twenty years since they had seen each other and their conversations since the IFYA disaster had been few, terse and angst-driven. Andrew watched Mei-Lien scan the crowds lining the customs exit and waved to her. As her eyes met his, she broke from her family. Supporting her belly, she half-walked, half-trotted following Andrew's waving hand. He skirted the cluster of waiting people and turned into an open area at the same time as Mei-Lien. Without hesitation, she embraced him and he enfolded her in his arms. She sobbed and whispered over and over, "Thank you, thank you."

Mrs. Zhang took her time pushing the luggage cart, surrounded by her grandchildren. As they moved into the open area, Mei-Lien let go of Andrew and wiped her eyes. Mrs. Zhang put her arm around his waist and he, her shoulder. They remained there and exchanged not a word, conveying the inexpressible.

"John Paul, Grace and Peter," said Mei-Lien, "This is our very good friend, Andrew."

~

The van was pulling up as the travellers pushed their luggage cart out of the sliding doors to the curb. The side door swung open and Emily flew out to embrace her mother. Rebecca assisted Amy to her mother's arms. Mei-Lien had her arms around both daughters, kissing one on the head and then the other. Grace, Peter and John Paul began hugging their sisters from behind, so Emily turned to hug each in turn and then her grandmother. Mei-Lien kept a strong grip on Amy, "Let's get you back into the van." Rebecca eased Amy to her seat and came out to help Mei-Lien. Mei-Lien extended her hand, but did not make a move to enter the van. Instead, she held Rebecca's hand and said, "You must be Rebecca."

"And you, Mei-Lien."

"Thank you for caring for my daughters," said Mei-Lien as she embraced Rebecca.

"Me? Look at what you are doing for them!" Rebecca whispered as she held Mei-Lien. "What courage you have."

"I don't feel very brave," Mei-Lien whispered back.

"Feeling courageous has nothing to do with courage," said Rebecca.

CHAPTER 79

The group had just arrived at Mrs. Zhang's when Mei-Lien's phone rang. She was expecting the call. On the way from the airport, as they neared her childhood home, she had texted Scott that Amy had been found. Mei-Lien signalled to her mother and whispered when she drew near, "It's him." Mei Lien followed her mother to the office at the front of the house. When Mrs. Zhang turned to leave, Mei-Lien motioned for her to stay and put the phone on speaker.

~

The children had never been to Grandma's house: she had always come to them. They wandered through the first floor like they were visiting a shrine, taking in everything, especially the pictures of their mother when she was a little girl. Then they split up, going upstairs and down to the finished basement. When Mei-Lien and her mother disappeared into the office, Micah and Andrew continued to prepare lunch and Rebecca settled Amy on the couch in the living room.

~

"Where are you?" demanded Scott.

"I could ask you the same," said Mei-Lien calmly.

"I came home, expecting to find my family and the place is deserted. Where are you?"

"I expected our agreement would be respected—the girls were not to go to the concluding ceremonies at the festival site. Where were you when our daughter was missing in that IFYA hellhole?"

"She's been found!"

"Yes, she's been found. By whom? By you? By the PoCs? No, by people my mother and I sent out to search for her while you dithered in Australia, too cowardly to call."

"Where are you, Mei-Lien?" Scott demanded.

"I suppose you found the empty safe."

Scott made no reply.

"Taking the extra key you so earnestly gave me—'Put it in a safe spot.' The duplicity! And hiding the passports under some fabricated false bottom?"

"It was for safe-keeping," responded Scott.

"No, it was for control," said Mei-Lien. Then lowering her voice, "Scott, it's over. I won't be coming back and neither will the children."

"You can't."

"Yes, I can. Both girls caught in the middle of a stampede! Amy, spending the night on the roadside, semi-conscious! That's where Amy was found, Scott—she crawled under a bush to get out of the fray. And all due to your reckless behaviour, your permission to disregard the explicit agreement we made before the trip. You endangered the lives of our daughters. I'm on my way to the doctor with both Emily and Amy. We are going to document every bruise, every injury, every inhumane experience to which they were subjected. It will all be documented."

"Amy's with *you*?"

"Yes, Scott, and Emily. I'm with my mother and all the kids in California. And this is where we will be staying."

Scott changed his tone. "Mei-Lien, come home," he soothed. "We can work this out."

Although Mei-Lien had no intention of returning to Scott, she marvelled at the allure of his voice, even after all she had been through.

"I know you've had a scare," he continued. "I'm sorry for that.

I should have called you sooner, I should have let you know I was coming home. Be the bigger person, Mei-Lien. Forgive and move on." Scott paused, letting his words sink in. Then, very tenderly he said, "You're going to have a baby soon. You're tired and over-sensitive . . . Mei, Mei, you know how easily you succumb to your emotions when you're expecting—"

"It's over, Scott" said Mei-Lien, unmoved. "My lawyer will be in contact with you as soon as we've ascertained the full extent of Emily's and Amy's trauma. And don't think of bringing out the big guns of the PoCs or I will sue you and them to the fullest extent of the law. The law, Scott. The law doesn't give a damn about the exhortations and decrees of the Founder but the law is very keen on neglect and endangerment."

Mei-Lien closed the line. "Do you know any family lawyers, Mom?"

CHAPTER 80

Rebecca drove Mei-Lien and her two older daughters to the doctor. Mei-Lien invited Rebecca into the examining room to document everything the doctor said and to photograph all injuries. When they returned to Mrs. Zhang's home in mid-afternoon, everyone went to bed and did not get up until the following morning.

Andrew, Micah and Rebecca stayed on another couple of days to help move furniture and assemble bunk beds. The children took turns going out with Grandma to pick up some clothes.

One by one, beginning with Emily, Mei-Lien explained to the children why they would now be living with Grandma and not their father. Mei-Lien was worried about Emily. Of all her children, she seemed to emulate her father the most. Emily was lively, bright, idealistic and a budding linguist. She was considered a natural leader and was highly regarded among the PoCs. Mei-Lien also felt Emily was being groomed to assume the translating that she herself had abandoned. However, Mei-Lien discovered that Emily's desire for her father's approval and, by extension, the PoCs, was shattered when she was forced to break her promise to her mother and Amy—a promise that she knew her dad and Nina had also agreed to. Emily had been as anxious to be reunited with Amy as Amy was with her. From their conversation, Mei-Lien could sense Emily's lingering shame and anguish over Amy's disappearance and her gratitude for her mother's efforts to reunite them.

Of all her children, Amy was the least perturbed about leaving her dad: she actually seemed relieved. Her reasons, however, disturbed Mei-Lien the most. "It will be better, Mom," Amy said. "Dad's always away and when he comes home, he bosses everyone around. And his friends are asses."

"Asses?"

"Some of them are mean to you."

"Were they mean to you?" she asked gently.

Amy put her head down. "They don't like me."

Given Amy's fragile state, Mei-Lien did not push her further but she was resolved to find out exactly what had happened in the past that evoked this response.

CHAPTER 81

"Rebecca, do you have forty bucks?" asked Andrew. "I owe Micah for some groceries he picked up."

Rebecca rummaged through her wallet. A slip of paper fell out. Unfolding it she asked, "What do you make of this, Andrew?"

"Where did it come from?"

"Amy's pants. Before throwing out her soiled clothes at the condo, I went through her pockets. We were in such a rush, I stuffed it in my wallet and forgot all about it."

On the paper were two names and numbers. One they recognized— Nina. The other, Cassandra, they did not. When they asked Mei-Lien, she was just as puzzled and Amy could not remember the name or how the paper got in her pocket.

"Rebecca, why don't you give her a call," said Mei-Lien, "and see if you can find out how she is connected to Amy. Use my mom's office. It's quieter there."

~

"Cassandra? Yes, this is Rebecca Holden. I was at the IFYA. We found your number in the back pocket of one of the participants. Were you also there?"

"As a medic . . . I don't usually give out my cellphone number. Who is the person?" she asked, distressed.

"Amy Tan."

"A young Chinese girl?"

"Yes."

"Oh, my God! Yes, I remember her. I wasn't able to remain with her. Is she okay?"

After assuring Cassandra that Amy was safely home with her mother, Cassandra choked up and began to recount what had happened. Rebecca interrupted, "Cassandra, may I record this? Her mother is quite concerned about what happened and Amy has not been able to remember very much."

With permission granted, Rebecca ran out of the office, grabbed Andrew's phone and recorded the medic's saga. As she was drawing to a close, Rebecca asked Cassandra about her own injury from the shrapnel.

"I was lucky and so was the young guy who was hit along with me. We were both struck in a muscle and not across a major blood vessel. We'll recover. But not everyone was so fortunate. Another girl was struck in the neck as she was fleeing and died before help arrived."

"What!" exclaimed Rebecca.

"Yes, it's appalling. I heard there have been four or five deaths and thousands and thousands of injuries—broken bones, sprains, collapse from exhaustion and dehydration, heart attacks, seizures, etc. etc. To make matters worse, the people injured don't have their medical records here. They speak every language under the sun and translators can't always be found—and frantic parents from all over the world are jamming the phone lines. It's an absolute mess—the hospitals are overwhelmed. You were fortunate to get out when you did."

~

"Andrew, you have to hear this," said Rebecca as she handed back his phone. "I need a copy of the recording and so does Mei-Lien." Then lowering her voice so as not to disturb the children who were in the kitchen, "Cassandra has contacts in the hospitals. She said there have been some deaths."

Andrew signalled to Micah and they moved into the living room and turned on a news channel. The weather report was up but the rolling strip of news on the bottom of the screen highlighted the IFYA disaster so they waited a few minutes for the newscast to begin. They were not disappointed.

Aerial views showed the deserted festival site studded with the trampled belongings of the participants and then cut to the tents set up in hospital parking lots to handle the throngs of injured participants. The anchor reiterated details that the three viewers were already well aware of. He then said, "While the final numbers are not yet in, four participants have been confirmed dead. The cause of death and the identification of the victims have not yet been released. And now we turn to our news reporter in the capital." The news reporter came on the screen, "Yes, I'm here in the capital getting responses from members of the Catholic Church on this tragedy. Here with me now is Rev. Theo O'Rourke."

"Theo!" exclaimed Micah.

"He's already in Washington!" said Andrew in disbelief.

Rebecca shushed them so they could hear what Theo had to say.

"In my conversations among the clergy here in the capital," Theo said solemnly, "there is agreement that the International Festival for Young Adults should be completely overhauled. While the IFYA has been an amazing success over the past years, this unfortunate event indicates the need for a fresh vision."

"What!" exploded Andrew and Micah.

"Unfortunate event!" exclaimed Rebecca, "It's a senseless, unnecessary disaster!"

"The dangers of the IFYA were apparent ages ago!" exclaimed Andrew. "And the template comes from Rome! I can't believe this! The downside of the IFYA has always been underreported: the sickness and injuries, the cost to the parishes and tax payers, the waste, the excessive travel, the garbage left behind, and God knows what else."

"The only wonder is that a tragedy like this hasn't happened before," added Rebecca. She flicked off the TV as the reporter babbled on with random passers-by.

"Theo! Of all people—the spokesperson for the reform of the IFYA," laughed Micah. "They should call him Teflon Theo."

"Your report should shed some light on the matter, Andrew," said Rebecca.

"Oh, I'll write the report," said Andrew, "but it'll be superfluous. The international investigation that's going to be carried out, the law suits . . ."

CHAPTER 82

"We'll be sorry to see you go," said Mrs. Zhang.

"We would never have been able to accomplish what we did without you," said Mei-Lien. "Just having you here these past couple of days made me feel safer."

The kids had settled early into their new bedrooms and beds. The adults were in the living room with iced tea or wine. The next morning Andrew, Rebecca and Micah were leaving. Since they were in California, they decided to spend a few days visiting family before Andrew and Rebecca flew back to Chicago and Micah returned to work.

"What did the lawyer say about the temporary custody order?" asked Rebecca.

"I have a court date for the end of this week," said Mei-Lien.

Beyond equipping and rearranging the house for Mei-Lien's large family, the preeminent concern of the past few days was ensuring Mei-Lien's custody of the children. Mrs. Zhang secured a divorce lawyer who had experience with cults, and she and Mei-Lien opened a safe deposit box for passports and other important documents. Rebecca helped Mei-Lien pull together the documentation the lawyer had requested. She also transcribed pertinent sections of the medic's testimony and made a digital copy of the entire phone conversation.

"Is the lawyer optimistic?" asked Micah.

"He thinks I have a good chance of eventually getting permanent custody and only supervised visits for Scott."

"He mentioned something about a parent's practice of religion causing actual harm to a child," said Mrs. Zhang, "and we certainly have proof of that."

"We have to wait and see how Scott counteracts," said Mei-Lien, apprehensively.

"Are you going to be okay financially?" asked Rebecca.

"We don't want his mon—" Mei-Lien and her mother both said together. Mrs. Zhang let Mei-Lien finish.

"We don't want his money, although I'm sure he's loaded. Supposedly, his parents, out of their love and beneficence, paid for our apartment and the private English school for our kids but I'm convinced it was part of the compensation for Scott's work. In our joint account we always had just enough money coming in every month, never enough to save for the future. It's nothing in comparison to the work Scott does—or my translations when that was happening. Though Scott's extended family are involved with commodities, he and his dad deal heavily in real estate. I wouldn't be surprised if he has properties throughout the world. I don't care. I don't want it. When I'm settled, I can work."

"You're going to have your hands full for a while with a new little one. I told you, I invested your dad's life insurance for you. You'll be okay." Then turning to the others in the room, "The lawyer said the custody hearings will go more smoothly without money involved."

"Besides," said Mei-Lien, "I don't think Scott is really interested in taking care of our children for any length of time. He sure hasn't shown any signs of that throughout our marriage."

"How so?" asked Andrew.

"I'd known it all along, I guess, but the awareness began to dawn when we were in Rome for the Pope's blessing. Because Scott was appointed coordinator of the Hong Kong delegation, our family had the 'distinct honour' of a private meeting between the Pope and all the coordinators with their families. We circled around a large room so that the Pope could shake hands with each family and have a picture with them. Throughout, Scott was all smiles, holding our youngest and jostling playfully with the others like the Father of the Year.

"As I watched, I realized how seldom I had seen Scott play or interact lightheartedly with the children. He was so jovial and at ease as he spoke with the Pope and the Pope was so profuse in his praise and good wishes. It struck me that Scott likes to be seen as a father of a big family, loves the image of it, but not so much the day-to-day work of it.

"So I started to track all his trips—for his father's business as well as the PoC's, and all the evening meetings—not including the ones we have to attend weekly as a family. I was right. He was literally gone more than half the time and hardly at home when he was home. I think that was one of the reasons Emily was getting so involved in the PoCs—to connect with her dad and win his approval.

"I doubt Scott is willing to curtail his international travel in order to have joint custody. Just the same, he'll probably put up a fuss . . . more out of a show of power, to flaunt who's boss."

"I'm still surprised he didn't come flying in the day after we did," said Mrs. Zhang.

"I think it's because he has to deal with the fallout of the fiasco at the IFYA. He and Nina organized the PoC contingent from Hong Kong and a number of the young people were from PoC Bible programs—their parents are not full-fledged members. They're half-baked members like my mom; they might cause trouble." She nudged her mother, sitting next to her on the couch. "Until all those kids are accounted for and reunited with their parents, I don't think we'll be seeing him. But the local PoCs will be circling."

"Which brings to mind," said Mrs. Zhang, "the holy of holies, our dearly beloved Founder seems to be uncommonly silent."

"Well, Mom, certain information is only shared among the 'Invested', not with the likes of you! And my name hasn't been banished from the email list . . . yet. This came in yesterday but I only read it this afternoon."

Mei-Lien picked up her phone, clicked open an email and read it.

Our Founder is deeply troubled by the recent occurrences at the IFYA. From the moment he heard the news, he confined himself to our regional retreat house. From the chapel on the ridge he gazes over the afflicted city and remains in constant prayer for all those injured. Like our Lord on the Mount of Olives, he suffers yet accepts the will of God.

The cause of the disaster was beyond anyone's power to control—a ferocious storm came out of nowhere. Yet our Founder tells us God will use this adversity to test our fidelity.

The Founder exhorts us to heed the words of Jesus and 'be wise as serpents.' The enemies of the Church will use this event to undermine faith in the Pope, the Vicar of Christ, and in his one, holy, Catholic Church. Negative words will become fodder for the devil's work. No one should speak with reporters or post on social media.

Likewise, there should be no murmuring among the PoC brothers and sisters. If you feel the need to talk about the untoward event, discuss it within the sacred confines of confession with a PoC priest or in strict confidence with a Guardian. These persons will bring your concerns to the Founder. Those in authority will review the event with the hierarchy.

The Founder will continue to pray for all those affected and asks them to offer their suffering for the conversion of sinners.

The pious dissembling in the email was so absurd it became hilarious to the weary group who listened. They laughed in disbelief, wiping away tears.

"I need more wine," said Andrew getting up to open another bottle.

CHAPTER 83

Resting back in their chairs, they sipped from their glasses.
"What a bizarre journey brought us all together," said
Mei-Lien.

"Don't you dare say, 'It was all according to God's plan,'" said Mrs.
Zhang. "I'm done with all that bullshit."

"No, no," Mei-Lien laughed. Then growing serious, "I walked into
a quagmire."

"I pushed you into the quagmire," said Mrs. Zhang with a sigh.

"You pushed me in that direction but the PoCs did the rest. I was
so naïve and confused, and taken in by their flattery, their certitude,
and the idealism of it all. I just got pulled in more and more."

"When did you begin to realize what was going on?" asked Rebecca
gently.

"I was told I was the model wife, an example for those in the
Movement and as well as those outside of it. After Grace, my fourth
child, I just couldn't fulfill all the demands the group was asking of me
and I stopped trying. At first, I considered myself a failure and then I
started to notice certain things. I guess I had noticed them before . . .
In Hong Kong the blinders fell off altogether. It's hard to explain . . . It's
not that you don't know. At some level, you're seeing, you're hearing,
you're feeling—you're comprehending it all. No, it's not that you don't
know. It's allowing yourself to admit what you know."

"But how can that be?" asked Micah. A straight-shooter throughout life, he could not comprehend how a person could evade reality to that degree.

"I guess," replied Rebecca, "it depends on how important the illusion is for the life you've built up, for the relationships you cherish . . . or just need to survive."

Mei-Lien nodded. "Who wants to admit they've been so stupid . . . that the sacrifices, extreme at times, were for nothing more than to fan another's ego and line his pockets," she said.

"God gets aligned with the leader: heaven is promised for following the Founder and the path to hell if you dare leave," continued Rebecca. "And when that Movement or group has been vetted and approved by the highest authority in the Catholic Church, more credibility is given to the leader and people doubt their perceptions even more."

"Then, once you're in a foreign country, you're isolated from extended family and friends," added Andrew shaking his head. "All your relationships are restricted to the Movement and its members in your local community. It's the perfect storm for control and abuse."

"I have my mom," said Mei-Lien, intertwining her arm in her mother's. "Could I have done this without her? Being in Hong Kong, with no money of my own? With the possibility of losing my kids?" Mei-Lien let out a sigh. "Even when you finally allow yourself to see, it's complicated."

"I was there to help, Mei-Lien, but *you* had to choose to stay in that quagmire or climb out. And perhaps in one of the worst moments of your life, you took the leap."

"Not knowing what happened to my daughters . . . then losing Amy," said Mei-Lien wistfully. "I don't think I would have had the courage to make the leap if not for the disaster at the festival."

"Often when life is the darkest we more clearly see the light," said Mrs. Zhang. "Like dawn through the shadows."

CHAPTER 84

A thick fog rolled through the college overnight. By midmorning it hovered above the campus like a dome. Mrs. Zhang and Fr. Hachette were setting up tables on the broad lawn that surrounded the college chapel. A small round table with a ceramic bowl, ewer and a vial of oil stood a few yards to the side.

Andrew and Rebecca pulled into the parking lot on the other side of the chapel.

"It's so quiet. Where are the students?" asked Rebecca.

"Saturday morning? They probably just went to bed!"

They were just stepping out of their rental car when a van tooted behind them. Raph and his partner, Jeff, pulled up with their adopted twins and Andrew's mom and dad, Sonia and Keith. After the hugs and greetings, the seven-year-old twins pulled Andrew and Rebecca to the back of the van where Jeff was pulling out trays of food. "Look what we brought. We helped daddy make them."

"What have we here?" asked Andrew as Jeff passed him a tray.

"Quiche bites," said Raph.

Jeff passed another tray to Rebecca, "Cobblers."

"And," said Raph as Jeff distributed the remaining trays and a bowl, "Miniature cinnamon buns, sticky mango rice balls, our signature fruit salad and steamed rolls."

Rebecca glanced at Andrew, "I don't think anyone is going to be interested in our store-bought fruit and veggie trays."

As the group made its way to the lawn on the other side of the chapel a bike swerved into the lot and the rider unsnapped his helmet. The twins ran to their Uncle Micah. "Spent the night at my sister's and borrowed her bike," said Micah as he joined the family. He swiped a quiche bite that was peeking out the corner of a tray.

"What the hell!" exclaimed Raph. "Stay out of that."

"If you're hungry you can nibble on these veggies," said Andrew, holding out the plastic container.

"Not after I just sampled this quiche from Jeff's kitchen," said Micah. Then looking at the fruit and veggie trays, "Where did you pick these up? At the dollar store?"

"What did you bring?" quipped Andrew.

"My good nature and charm!"

"That's my boy," said Sonia.

"You've been usurped," said Rebecca to Andrew.

As the family group rounded the corner, Mrs. Zhang smiled with delight and began to greet her guests. Raph and Jeff were arranging the trays at a table when Mrs. Zhang came up from behind and hugged both at the waist. "Thank you for preparing all this. It looks wonderful. But you must let me pay you!"

"No, Mrs. Z," said Raph. "This is our gift to you and your new granddaughter."

Just then John Paul, Peter and Grace came charging around the chapel and into the arms of Rebecca, Micah, Andrew and Sonia. Peter remained near Sonia, hugging her leg. Sonia met Mei-Lien and her family during a brief visit when she was driving Rebecca and Andrew back to the airport in July. A relationship developed. Sonia stayed with the family as Mei-Lien approached her due date and remained until after the birth. She and Peter had a special bond.

Emily, Amy and Mei-Lien, carrying her infant daughter, now walked toward the group. The twins peered at the tiny baby, allowing her to curl her hand around their fingers. After the children were introduced to each other, Hachette gathered everyone near the round table. Mei-Lien wanted her daughter baptized but every time she entered a church she felt like she was suffocating, so Hachette arranged the ceremony outside. "After all, Jesus was baptized in a river," he said.

Mei-Lien passed her daughter to the godparents, Rebecca and Andrew, who were standing to the side of Hachette. Rebecca cradled the infant while Andrew stood with his arm around her shoulder. Mei-Lien and her mother stood on the other side of Hachette facing the encircled group of family and friends.

"What name do you give to your child?" asked Hachette as he began the rite.

"Rebecca Andree," replied Mei-Lien.

~

After the baptism, Emily and Amy spread out blankets on the lawn near a large black oak while Hachette, Keith and Andrew pulled out a few chairs. The adults sat and chatted as they ate and little Becky was passed from arm to arm. The children picked out their favourite foods and ate while they played with the bubbles that Mei-Lien had bought for the occasion. Emily was the most popular with a giant bubble wand. Amy took to the twins, holding their bottles of sudsy fluid and giving them tips on bubble blowing. Jeff circled around with his trays of food and Raph followed with a fruit punch. Andrew sat leaning against the ancient tree, Rebecca in his arms holding Becky. The fog swirled above them, sometimes sending down wisps, like incense, that curled among them. The circle of adults continued to converse and the children laughed and skipped about, unruffled by the shrouded sky.

ACKNOWLEDGEMENTS

Although writing is a solitary venture, the birth of a book is never accomplished alone. I am grateful to the many persons who have helped make *Dawn Through the Shadows* a reality. Special thanks to:

My brothers, sisters and extended family for their love, support and enthusiastic promotion of my novels.

To my sisters, Nikki and Kimi, and my niece, Lisa, who read through my drafts (Nikki, more than once and with a sharpened pencil).

To my brother, Anthony, who assists with technical details.

To Helen and Colin MacIsaac for their friendship, continual encouragement and willingness to read my drafts.

To Rosalyn Schmidt, my copyeditor, for her meticulous reading of my manuscript and for her friendship over the years.

To Erik Mohr, my cover artist and interior designer, for capturing the essence of *Dawn Through the Shadows* in his dramatic cover. His intriguing art on *Terrifying Freedom* contributed to many book club discussions.

To the booksellers and librarians who have recommended my books. A very special thanks to Tami Grondines for her belief in my novels and for opening doors for in-store book signings.

To all the readers who have shared their reflections with me. I've been blessed by your insights and the stories of your own life journeys. Thank you.

BIO

Linda Smith lives near Calgary, Alberta, engaging with children as an educational assistant and enjoying the beauty of the Rocky Mountains.